FIREWEED

FIREWEED

Jill Paton Walsh

HOT
KEY
BOOKS

Published in Great Britain in 2013 by Hot Key Books
Northburgh House, 10 Northburgh Street, London EC1V 0AT

First published by Macmillan & Co. Ltd in 1969

A CIP catalogue record for this book is available
from the British Library.

ISBN: 978-1-4714-0174-9

4

Typeset by Palimpsest Book Production Limited, Falkirk,
Stirlingshire
This book is typeset in 11/15.9pt Sabon

Printed and bound by Clays Ltd, Elcograf S.p.A

FSC

Hot Key Books supports the Forest Stewardship Council (FSC), the
leading international forest certification organisation, and is
committed to printing only on Greenpeace-approved FSC-certified
paper.

www.hotkeybooks.com

Hot Key Books is part of the Bonnier Publishing Group
www.bonnierpublishing.com

Foreword by Lucy Mangan

To this day I cannot believe this is how we did it, but it's true. At school our English classes – that's seven or eight hours every week, for years and years and years – were devoted to reading books aloud. Whole books. Aloud. Every word. Three or four pages per pupil, round and round we went, from *The Starlight Barking* and *The Phantom Tollbooth* in our first year, through the likes of *Bridge to Terabithia* in pre-GCSE years and then on to *Pride and Prejudice. Lord of the Flies. 1984. Wuthering Heights* (*Wuthering Heights*. Aloud. WUTHERING HEIGHTS) in the awful GCSE and downright hellish A-level years. Few pupils, and even fewer books, survived the experience.

One book that did, however, was Jill Paton Walsh's *Fireweed*. Partly, it must be said, because of its relative brevity. It simply didn't hang around long enough to become a burden on your soul like that Brontë monstrosity did.

But more than that – it spoke to us, a classful of twelve-year-olds, who were just beginning to feel the stirring of longings for independence, adventure and romance (or sex, as we called it, not knowing any better). The gradual unfolding of the love story between Bill, an unhappy evacuee during the Second World War who returns to London to fend for himself until his soldier father comes home, and Julie, a fellow fugitive whom he meets while sheltering in a tube station during an air raid fed, like all the best and best-timed books do, a need in us we didn't even know we had.

I simply loved it, this short, surefooted tale of life, love and London in the Blitz. It was the first book I had read that seemed to be conveying more than it actually said (and yes, E. Brontë, I'm looking at you. Again). I took it home and re-read and re-read it, unpacking a little more of its clever, compact subtleties each time but always, in the end, simply getting caught up in Bill and Julie's adventures, hopes, happiness and bitter disappointments as they make their way through the capital's wartime chaos and pull a life from the rubble of their pre-war certainties and expectations. They build their own tiny world together while London is, as Bill puts it, 'knocked to blazes' all around them.

Thus it was that the ending – oh, that ending! – managed to catch me off guard every time and break my heart anew. As London shatters, Bill's feelings for Julie deepen and flourish like the fireweed that takes root in the bombsites all over the city. Then, when Julie is eventually injured and hospitalised, her parents find her, and the intrusion of adults and their all-consuming concerns about class and propriety destroy Bill's fragile idyll. He is banished from her room and, despite her mother's brief flicker of sympathy ('You know, Bill – she's only a child'), from her life thereafter.

Had I been a year or two younger when I read it I would have writhed in rage at the bittersweet conclusion of Bill's story. As it was, I was just old enough to begin to appreciate the tender art of yearning and wriggle in delight instead at the exquisite pain involved. Now that I am older still, I feel the same but can delight almost as much in the artistry and the careful, elegant but vitally unobtrusive language involved in bringing us all to that pitch and that delicate, fragile emotion to life.

A few years ago, I discovered that the author herself does not remain so enamoured of her work. I was at a lecture in Cambridge on children's literature and afterwards someone pointed out Jill Paton Walsh to me. I had had just enough white wine to give me the courage to tell her how much I loved her book.

The author listened to whatever idiotic fragments of introduction and explanation made it out of my mouth and then proceeded to tell me briskly (I remembered then that she had been a teacher before turning to writing for a living) that she did not like the book at all any more, that the parents' intervention was crass ('They seemed to come from another book') and that although she had considered it all right at the time, she now looked on it more or less as juvenilia.

Suitably chastened, I slunk away. But later my marginally mutinous teenage self rose and said – though not out loud – 'So what?' A book belongs as much to the reader as to the author and to my mind, then and now, the eruption of the parents into Bill and Julie's lives seemed only an exaggerated reflection of the many daily unwanted and to teenage minds unwarranted intrusions of parents into one's own life. They are a bombshell on their own, the breaking of a dream, a brutal reassertion of real life – and what young person hasn't experienced that and burned with resentment of it? Bill's embittered flames burn hotter and longer and with more just cause, but they are fed and fanned by the same teenage passions.

So my battered, beloved old copy from 1986 remains proudly on my bookshelf – soon to be joined by this rather more prepossessing copy – and I still both remember and re-read it with fondness and a small, sweet knife in the heart as it draws to a close. I hope that this new edition will be taken down and read by a new generation who find it as illuminating, moving and rewarding as I have done for the last twenty-odd years. Ideally, not at school. And very definitely not aloud.

For my father-in-law

My thanks are due to almost everyone I know who is old enough to remember 1940; to many other authors whose work I have consulted, and to Miss Elizabeth Almung, who gave me invaluable assistance.

J.P.W.

1

Remember? I can still smell it. I met her in the
Aldwych Underground Station, at half past six in
the morning, when people were busily rolling up
their bedding, and climbing out to see how much
of the street was left standing. There were no
lavatories down there, and with houses going down
like ninepins every night there was a shortage of
baths in London just then, and the stench of the
Underground was appalling. I noticed, as I lurked
around, trying to keep inconspicuous, that there
was someone else doing the same. I was lurking
because I wanted to stay in the warm for as long
as possible, without being one of the very last out,

in case any busybody asked me tricky questions. And there was this girl, as clearly as anything, lurking too.

I was fifteen that year, and she seemed sometimes younger, sometimes older. She looked older now, because she had that air adults have, of knowing exactly what they are doing and why. Now I come to think of it, lurking is the wrong word for her; *I* was lurking – she was just staying put. But I knew she was playing some game like mine, because she hadn't any bedding either. She was clever at getting out unnoticed. She waited till a great loudly-yapping family with kids all sizes came swarming past her, and then just tagged along behind them. I joined their wake too. Mum and Dad were staggering under so many blankets they might perfectly well have been carrying ours too.

When we trudged up the steps to street level, she looked around her. So did everyone else. There was always less damage than you would think. This time, as far as I recall, the street looked the same as it had done the night before. She wasn't looking for bomb-damage though, she was wondering which way to go. I went along beside her and said 'Hello'.

She just glanced at me, and then went hurrying on, looking straight ahead of her, but that quick glance stopped me in my tracks for fully sixty seconds. There was no mistaking the expression in them. She was terrified. She was running now, down towards the Law Courts. But when some bowler-hatted Johnnie turned round to look at her she slowed up, and went in a trotting sort of walk, sidling through the people, not looking back. I went after her. I don't really know why.

She left the Strand, and went down into the warren of little streets between the Strand and the river. I lost her for a bit, so I slowed up, and looked around. There was a great crater in the Strand, with the cars going gingerly round the edge of it. There were a lot of new shrapnel holes in the pavement, and across the river there were still fires burning on the South Bank. Down towards Charing Cross an ambulance bell wailed shrilly.

I found her again sitting on a bench in the Embankment Gardens. I came up behind the bench so she shouldn't see me, and then stepped smartly round, and stood right in front of her, so she couldn't very easily jump up and run away.

'Hullo,' I said. 'What did you run away for?'

She looked up at me, eyes wide. 'I'm cold,' she said in a shaky voice. 'I want something hot to drink.'

'Sorry,' I said. 'I haven't any money.' I was down to my last sixpence.

'I have. Take me and buy some breakfast.' I just looked at her. 'You can have some too, if you take me,' she said.

I was very hungry. Too hungry to turn her down, but I didn't feel like leaving it at that.

'Why did you run away?' I asked. She looked at me coldly, with large brown eyes.

'I didn't know what sort of boy you were,' she said. 'You might have been anybody,'

'I *am* anybody,' I protested.

'You'll do all right for taking me to have some breakfast,' she said.

'Thanks,' I said, crossly. 'Why don't you go by yourself?'

'Girls don't go around by themselves like that,' she said. 'And anyway, I don't know where to go.'

'Well, how much money have you got?' I thought of all the eating-places I knew near by.

'Plenty for bacon and eggs,' she said. My mouth watered embarrassingly at the thought.

'Wizzo!' I said. 'I'll take you.'

'Hold my hand,' she said, getting up.

'Why?'

4

'So that we look like brother and sister. Then nobody will ask us what we're doing by ourselves.'

'Brother and sister, *holding hands?*' I said, disgustedly, but then she looked as though she might be going to cry, and her hand was still held out towards me, so I took it, quickly.

'If you start crying all over the Embankment, that really *will* look inconspicuous,' I said icily. Then I relented a bit (well, I hadn't had anyone to talk to for days and days, and I couldn't keep up the iciness). 'You don't have to worry,' I told her, 'I've been doing it for a week, and nobody has noticed yet!'

'Doing what?'

'Getting along on my own, with no grown-ups,' I said. 'Like you're trying to.'

'Have you really?' she said, suddenly grinning at me. 'How terrific! How do you do it?'

'Oh, I have things worked out,' I told her, loftily, not wanting to throw away my moment of glory. 'I'll tell you later.'

'It must be easier for you,' she said, as we crossed out of the gardens and began to walk up towards the Strand again.

'Why must it?' I asked, annoyed at her for being disparaging.

'Well, you're a boy, after all, and then, well you see, *I've* run away!'

'So have I,' I retorted. 'And if you think it's so easy, I suppose you won't want me to tell you how it's done!'

I thought she would fall off her high-horse at that, and say 'Please tell me, oh, please', but she said, 'Anyway it will be easier with two of us.'

'You've got the hell of a cheek!' I told her.

'You haven't any money for breakfast,' she said, and that was true, and there we were at the door of Marco's Cosmopolitan Snack-Bar, and the heavy warm smell of frying and coffee was wafting round us.

I glared at her, and she said 'Pax. What's your name?'

'Bill,' I said. That isn't my name, but I decided in that split second to lie about it just in case, and then I couldn't bring myself later to admit I'd not trusted her, and tell her my real one. 'What's yours?'

'Julie,' she said.

'Ciao, ciao!' called Marco, as we went in. 'I was worried about you, amico. Where did you eat yesterday?'

'Oh, I was the other end of town, Marco. Too

far to come,' I said. I didn't like to say I had run out of money.

'Listen,' said Marco, his accent getting thicker as he spoke with feeling. 'As long as you know – anything you want, you ask Marco. I get you good food, I ask no questions, I not even *think* questions. So long as you know. I am your friend, Marco, your big friend.'

'Thanks Marco, I know. Bacon and eggs for two, and a cup of tea . . .'

'Coffee for me,' said Julie.

'Ah!' said Marco. 'Is good. Is better to have coffee. Black or white, Miss . . . Miss?'

'Julie,' she said. 'White please.'

'White coffee for Miss Julia,' he said, with a flourish. For a moment I thought she looked a bit startled. As soon as he moved away from the table she said, 'Is he all right? Is he really your friend?'

'He's all right. He's not really a friend. But he guessed I was up to something, because I came here so much on my own. He's jolly sore about having been interned as an enemy alien, because he's lived here years and years, and only had another few weeks to go for his naturalization to come through. Or so he says. They let him out again though, so I suppose that's true. But the whole business made him very angry. He says he doesn't like people who push people around, so I reckon he's on our side.'

Marco brought bacon and eggs, and tea for me, and coffee for her. My tea was in the usual thick white cup with brown chips on the rim, but he brought Julie's coffee in a pot, with a jug of hot milk, and a blue cup, unchipped.

'Thank you,' she said, smiling.

I remember seeing that she was smiling very nicely, and realizing that this was why her cup wasn't a chipped one. I was a bit rueful as I gulped my lukewarm tea, but I tucked into that plate of bacon and eggs gladly enough.

'It's jolly nice in its way, but it doesn't taste quite the same, somehow,' I said thoughtfully, mopping up yellow egg-yolk with a chunk of bread.

'He cooks in olive oil,' she said.

'You are my friends,' said Marco, appearing to pour more coffee into Julie's cup, though she could perfectly well have done that herself as far as I could see. 'For you, I cook in the olive oil. Only the best for you.'

A few more people were straggling into the place: two air-raid wardens in tin hats, and some workers on their way between shelters and work.

'You stay here as long as you like,' said Marco. 'You sit, you drink coffee, no hurry, plenty room.'

'Tell me about running away,' said Julie, looking at me over the coffee pot.

I told her a bit. I can't really remember how much. After all this time it's no good trying to remember just what I said; when I try to remember I remember very clearly what it was like, what I might have told her; and I remember trying to impress her, thinking that if I made out that I had had a rough time she would see what a brave, tough type I was. And pathetic though it seems to me now, I think I really did think things had been rough.

I hadn't really understood about war. Grown-ups talked about it, and they listened to the news more than they had done before. I liked spotting planes; I learned from the *Boy's Own Paper* what all ours, and all theirs, looked like, fighters and bombers, but it didn't mean anything much to me. I was living with my aunt. She had looked after me and my father since my mother died. I don't think she really wanted to, because she grumbled a lot. My father was still at home the first time they started sending children out of London. Evacuees, they called them. My class at the school went half empty one day; then there was only me and one other boy; then there was no class at all. The school closed down, and the teachers went off to the country to teach the kids there. My aunt wanted to send me too, but my father said 'The family stays together', and went on saying it steadily until she stopped talking about sending me away. So I stayed put.

It was deadly dull. I did a lot of shopping for her, and I was so bored I was glad to. It used up a lot of time, because there were suddenly queues at a lot of the shops. You had to register with one shop for things that were rationed, and that meant you couldn't go somewhere else if the queue was long.

The funny thing about the war was that nothing at all happened for ages and ages. All those kids had been sent away, and then there were no bombs at all. Now and then I saw a Hurricane, or Spitfire fly over our quiet street, and once I saw a Heinkel, but it was just flying over, not doing anything. Like everyone else in the street we got an Anderson shelter, a great package of bits of corrugated iron. We put it up in the garden, and covered it with earth, Dad and me working together the whole weekend. When it was finished he went round to the pub, and brought back a jug of beer, and we sat in the kitchen, and he poured some out for me. My aunt was furious, and nagged him about giving it to me, because I was too young.

'He's done a man's work today,' my father said. I didn't like the beer, but just to show her, I drank rather a lot. It made me sick, and while I was hanging over the bathroom basin my aunt appeared from her bedroom, in curlers, and yelled 'I told you so!' all over the place.

Sometime that summer my Dad's call-up papers came and he went off into the army. My aunt grumbled more than ever. He didn't write; he was never much good at putting words to things.

Then when they started putting up posters again, and making appeals on the wireless to send children out of London, my aunt decided to send me. I was furious; two of my best friends had just come back.

'You're going off with the rest of them this time,' she said to me. 'It's too dangerous here.'

I remember her saying that. I was standing with my back to her, looking out of the front room window. The street was sunlit, and the roses were blooming all over the front gardens. A horse stood outside the next door house, between the shafts of the milk cart, peacefully champing in his nosebag. The milkman was out of sight, but I could hear the chink of bottles.

'Dangerous?' I said. 'Here?' Suddenly her dry hard voice changed. She sounded wild as she answered,

'It's too much for me, do you hear? *You* are too much for me! You argue, and cheek me, and won't do what you're told, and eat more than I can buy on your ration book, and I can't keep track of you at all. You go out, and I never know where you are, and *you* don't care at all! What would it be like having you to worry about when the bombing starts? It's little enough you care about it. You just want to have a good time, as if it was nothing to you, as if there wasn't a war on! Well, you can just get out of it, and someone else can worry about you. I might be able to keep out of the line of a bomb, if I've only myself to take care of!' By the time she'd finished all this, she was crying, sniffing into her handkerchief.

I'd never really liked her. Looking back now, I can see that a great growing boy must have been a trial to a spinster with a small house, and not as much money as she had been used to, and getting on now, going grey, getting slower around the house. I didn't think of that then. I turned on her, furious.

'Before you send me anywhere,' I said, shouted rather, 'you ought to write to my father, and ask him!'

'I have written,' she said. 'I've told him that you've gone. Posted it this morning.'

The ground was slipping from under my feet. 'You old bitch!' I yelled at her.

'I was right,' she said. 'You *are* unmanageable. It's a good thing you're going. For your own sake. And you are not, ever, to talk to me like that again.'

'If I can't talk to you how I like, I'm not going to talk to you at all!' I said.

'Please yourself,' she snapped.

So that's how it was. We spent the next two days in utter silence, not saying anything to each other, even at mealtimes. She never read anything, but she could stare at the salt cellar all through a meal, till it nearly gave her a squint. It was a china salt cellar, with a few mauve flowers painted on it, now half rubbed off with age. I read, or pretended to read, *Kidnapped*. But though it was open in front of me, beside my plate, I had a head full of rage and scarcely read a word. John and Peter had only just been allowed to come home from their evacuee billets, and now I was being sent off; I'd have no friends left at all.

I felt angry the whole two days, and it never occurred to me how badly I was hurting myself, quarrelling with her just then. Still, that's how it was, and in the end I left without making it up with her, although she did give me a cold quick peck on the cheek on the platform at Paddington. And of course she was right that the war didn't mean anything to me, that I took no notice of it at all. I left her without even asking for my Dad's address; she didn't know where I was going, of course, and she left me without any money at all, not even a penny for a stamp to write home with.

The whole station was crammed with kids. Some were in proper groups with teachers looking after them, some were odd bods like me. We all had little bags with a change of clothes, and luggage labels pinned on our chests, with name and address written on them in capitals. My spare clothes were in a carrier bag, with 'Harvey's Drapery' on it. Some of the kids were very little, and a few of them were howling, enough to make an awful noise, though most of them just looked blank, or frightened. There were a lot of bossy grown-ups thrusting around yelling at people, and a few parents, shut away behind the barriers at the end of the platforms, waving, and jumping up and down trying to see.

A train came in, and filled up with kids, and pulled slowly away, filling the station with a thin haze of smoke, and looking like some sort of cater-pillar, with waving arms for legs. Then another train came in, and took almost everyone, but not me, or a few others who had been hanging back. Then a whole lot of girls trooped onto the platform, all wearing uniforms, and carrying twice as much as the rest of us. They were even humping hockey sticks. Some of them looked very young too. One small dark-haired girl began to grizzle just in front of me, and a great fat woman dressed all in blue hairy tweed, even to her hat, bore down on her, and slapped her back, and said loudly, 'Chin up, Harriet, mustn't let the side down!' Just then the porters started calling to us to board the train, and so I finished up in a carriage full of little girls, with this large tweedy woman facing me in the corner. She took off her coat, and put it on the luggage rack, and sat down and glared at me.

'I don't know what you think *you're* doing here, young man,' she said. She was wearing one of those nasty brooches made out of a bird's foot with the

15

claws still on. 'I think it's most unsuitable,' she added.

'Where are we going? Do you know?' I asked her. She looked as if there wasn't anything she didn't know.

'Don't ask questions!' she snapped. 'Don't you know there might be a Jerry listening, anywhere?'

'Well there isn't one here, unless it's you,' I thought, and sat and hated her while the train jerked its way out of the station.

We were in that train the whole day. She never said a kind word to any of her kids, but she certainly knew how to look after them. Her enormous bag had books in it, and spare handkerchiefs, and a bag of barley-sugar, and round about lunch-time she went up the corridor, and came back with piles of cheese sandwiches. When they had all finished eating in front of me, with me looking out of the window swallowing, trying not to look as hungry as I felt, she suddenly said, 'Have you anything to eat, young man?'

'No, Ma'am,' I said.

'Well, as good luck would have it,' she said, 'I have miscounted, and I find we have more sandwiches than we require. Here they are. You may have them.'

'Thanks, I mean thank you,' I said. She handed them over, unsmiling.

We passed station after station, but we didn't know where we were going because all the names were blacked out. At last we got somewhere, and people got out, and stood about on the platform. All the uniformed girls and their teachers collected together, and got shepherded out, and then they didn't know what to do with the rest of us. They uncoupled one carriage, and ordered us back onto that, and shunted it off into a siding. We waited half an hour, and then another train came in, with children's staring faces at all the windows, and they put our carriage onto the back of that train, and on we went. By now it was getting dark. It was pitch dark when we finally arrived.

Wartime dark was quite fearful, because of blackout regulations. They would have extinguished moon and stars, and set wardens over them if they could have. All lesser lights were put out. We all scrambled out of the carriages onto a strange platform, without even a torch to go by. I could hear adult voices somewhere up the platform, though I couldn't understand them. We stumbled against one another, groping in the thick night. Then the station master came up with

17

a lantern, heavily hooded, and walked up and down.

'How many are there, then?' called someone.

'Over a hundred, easy,' he answered. They had warm, sing-song voices. We were in Wales.

'Bring them through here,' the voice called. 'Let us count them over.'

Counted, we filed out of the station. It was not quite so dark under the open sky. There were people standing there, who seemed to have come to meet us. A man with a handful of papers in his hand was talking.

'More of them, see. I have got names of all those who offered to take them, and there are not enough places, not nearly. And late it is, already. Now everyone take some children, and go and find them billets. Not all the same way. We shall have to knock on all the doors till we find billets for all of them . . .'

There were a few minutes of great confusion, and then we were trudging uphill, stumbling, two by two, hand in hand. My hand was clutched by a tiny clammy paw belonging to a small boy, or perhaps a small girl, I couldn't see in the dark. Whoever it was was tired, pulled at me, hanging back, and whimpered a bit when it stumbled.

Every few steps we stopped, and the man with us knocked on a door. He spoke in Welsh, urgently. They looked out at us, peering into the darkness from their doorways, looking us over. We couldn't understand a word, yet it was easy to tell whether they were saying yes or no. Several times the man pushed me forwards, and the woman shook her head, and said something, and took a small child, much younger. I was nearly full grown by then, head and shoulders taller than the others in the group. At last I was the only one left, and he scratched his head a bit, and then took me up a rough track, still uphill, on and on, and then when I thought I couldn't walk a step further, he brought me through a yard of some kind, and knocked on a door. The woman who came said no, like all the others when she saw me, but he talked and talked, and then a man came to the door too, and joined in. Then suddenly the man who had brought me from the station left, and trudged away down the hillside, and they let me in through their door.

It was a big farm kitchen I walked into. A great log fire was burning in the chimney corner, and there was bread and cheese, and a cold roast chicken on the table. I was so hungry the sight of food made me feel tight in the stomach. They looked at me, and the man said something in Welsh.

'How old is it you are?' she asked me, in English.

'Fifteen,' I said.

'You look more. I thought you were a grown man when you stood out in the dark there,' she said. 'Will you want your bed right away?'

'Can I have something to eat first?' I asked.

'Right away, boy. Sit down then,' she said. She put food in front of me, four sorts of bread, and great hunks of cheese, and butter with beads of saltwater shining in it, and the rest of the chicken. She sat down by the hearth, and folded her hands in her lap, and the two of them talked together in Welsh. I listened to all that musical mumbo-jumbo and ate and ate, and as soon as I stopped feeling hungry my head drooped forwards onto my hands, and I fell asleep at the table where I sat.

2

I suppose I stuck it there for about five weeks. They weren't unkind; but Mr Williams, the farmer, spoke no English, only Welsh, and his two shepherds, David and Evans, were the same, save for a word or two. Mrs Williams, and their son, Hugh, could speak some English, enough to tell me simple things, like where to put my clothes to dry when I came in soaking, and when to come to table, and not to go by myself on the mountain; now and then they even talked to each other in a funny sort of English, just to help me not to feel left out of it. It didn't make me feel that! Anyway they couldn't manage it for long.

The farm was a mile above the village, on a narrow track all its own. The village wasn't like an English village at all; it had no church, but two chapels, one made of red brick, the other of green-painted corrugated iron, a bit rusty at the corners. There weren't any cottages, only rows of terraced houses like bits of a town thrown down in the valley, and ugly bits of a town at that: grey, and vicious red brick under slate tiles that seemed shiny with rain all the time. A railway ran up to the head of the valley, but it only served the slate quarry, where everyone worked who didn't work on a farm. For the rest there was mountain, great humps of bare green; smeared with blotches of purple where heather grew, blotting out the sides of the sky in every direction. And the colours and shapes of the land were always blurry, washed out by a haze of incessant fine rain. I suppose it can't have rained without stopping for five weeks, but that's how I remember it. I spent a lot of time lying on my bed, reading the only thing I could find – old *Woman's Weeklies*, with sloppy stories in them, which Mrs Williams kept stacked up under the stairs. They didn't seem to take a newspaper, and if they talked about the war, well, of course, I couldn't understand what they said.

Once the billeting officer came to see if I was giving any trouble, and they said no, thank you, they could manage me nicely. I plucked up courage to ask him if there was a school I could go to.

'There is the school in the village, boy,' he said. 'But nobody still at it, the age you are.'

'I was at a Grammar school,' I said. 'I should be at a Grammar school.'

'There is a Grammar school over the mountain, in Bala,' said Mrs Williams.

'He would have to go on the bus every morning, and come back at night,' said the billeting officer.

'Who would be paying for that, now?' asked Mrs Williams, 'And with books, and uniform too.'

He lowered his voice to a hoarse whisper. 'How about his family, do you think?'

'It is not like Mrs Jones's boy, who gets pocket money from home every week, as I hear. There has not been twopence for him yet. And he has no good boots, and no thick socks with him either, and his things only in a paper bag, too. I don't think it likely.'

And there they let it rest.

I swallowed my pride, and wrote a letter to my aunt. I told her about the school over the mountain, and asked her to tell my father. I asked her to let me have my father's address, and some money for stamps. Mrs Williams said I must wait till market day for a penny-halfpenny from her to post this letter; most days of the week she had no money with her. I daresay that was true, though at the time I thought she was being purposely cruel. Evan took pity on me, and gave it to me out of a box he kept on the chimneypiece, but he made me earn it by sweeping out the yard, and carrying wattle for a sheep-pen up to him on the hillside.

I took my letter down to the post office at the back of the village shop, and waited for an answer. And none came. Day after day went by, and no letter. I didn't even see the postman. In the valley bottom, along by the stream, the trees turned pale gold, and thinned so that chinks of sky showed through their branches. Evan and David and Hugh went up on the mountain every day, with the dogs, and brought down the sheep, and put them in the fields below the farm, where they bleated all day. I liked watching the dogs working, running round the sheep. But every day was spoiled at the start on which no letter came. I thought my aunt was still keeping up that silly quarrel we had had, and punishing me for calling her names. I hated her bitterly, worse every day.

Then one afternoon Mrs Williams hung up her apron behind the kitchen door, and put on a black hat, and a black coat with a fur collar, and went down to the village for a meeting, something to do with the chapel. She was gone all afternoon. I thought she looked at me a bit oddly when she came back. After supper she got a bowl of hot water, and a bar of black soap, and a funny fine comb, and set them one end of the kitchen table. I thought she was going to wash the dog. I took no notice.

'Come here, boy,' she said to me.

'What do you want?' I said, looking with suspicion at her broad aproned chest, and rolled-up sleeves.

'Come here, boy. I am just going to look at your head.'

'Look at my head? What the hell do you mean!'

'No need to fly off at me. Mrs Jones, and Mrs Evans both say their evacuees had lice. Now I am just going to clean you up, see?'

I backed away from her. 'You're not going to touch me!' I said.

'I will not have lice in my house,' she declared, 'no matter who it is they are on.'

'There aren't any lice in your house!' I said,

swaying between outrage and laughter. Watching us from his rocking chair by the fire, Mr Williams grinned broadly. I collected myself, and said in a normal tone, 'There are no lice in my hair, Mrs Williams, I have never had lice.'

'You just come here, boy, and let me see,' she said, marching towards me, comb in one hand, soap in the other. I tipped up a chair in front of her, and backed out through the door to the yard.

Evan and David were out there, with a lantern in the dusk, rolling a three-gallon drum back to the shed. She came to the door, and called out to them to stop me, or I suppose that's what she was calling, for they ran after me. I jumped over the wall into the field, and ran across the grass. Sheep lumbered away from me, bleating, as I went. Shouting gibberish at me the two shepherds came down the slope behind me.

At the bottom of the field there was a dip – a sort of narrow concrete pool, with a little stream running alongside it. Last time I had seen it the dip had been empty and dry. When I felt the hard concrete under my feet, I jumped, expecting to land on the bank of the stream, and be over that too in another stride. But the concrete was wet; I slipped, fell, and plunged into five feet of stinking water. The stink was heavy disinfectant. It reeked. It burnt my nose and mouth. I coughed, sank again, and took another mouthful. There was no grip on the sides of the pool, and the top edge was too high for me to reach. I floundered. Coming up with the lantern David and Evan stood high above my head on dry land, and laughed like maniacs, hanging on to each other for support, and howling with laughter. Somehow I struggled to the end of the pool, and scrambled out.

I was so angry I thought I was going to murder them. I caught myself looking round for a stone, and feeling the blow in my mind's eye. When I took a grip on myself I began to shake all over.

They were very concerned. They hurried me up to the farm house, and stood me beside the fire, while they peeled off my sodden clothes. I was still possessed by fury.

'What in hell was that there for?' I asked through my teeth.

'It's for delousing sheep, see,' said Hugh, roaring with laughter again. But I didn't think it was funny.

'I'm going to bed,' I said, clutching the towel I was wrapped in.

'Mrs Jones told me there is a letter for you at the Post Office, and you have not been asking for it,' said Mrs Williams. I stopped on the bottom step.

'You mean, someone has been keeping my letters?' I demanded.

'Keeping them back? You are not in London now, boy. The postman cannot come round the whole mountain, just for one or two letters for the farms. Our letters stay at the Post Office till we fetch them.'

Well, how could I have known that?

First thing next morning, I was down there, asking for it. Mrs Jones gave me two letters, out of a cubby hole behind the counter. I felt self-conscious, standing there, for I was sure I still smelt like a sheep, though I had stood in the yard for ten minutes pumping cold water over myself, and scrubbing down my flinching and tingling skin. I went out and sat on the stile opposite to read them.

The first was from my aunt. She thought being on a farm would be good for my health. She hoped I was being a good boy. She sent me my father's address, and a book of stamps, and hoped I would write to him often . . . I felt sorry I had been hating her. She must have sent the address on my letter to my father right away, too, because the other

28

letter was from him. He said things weren't too bad in the army, but he missed me a lot. He hoped I was not being more trouble than I could help to the people I was with. He had some leave coming soon, and would be spending it with my aunt, but it wouldn't seem like home without his boy. I was to spend the money how I liked. I looked in the envelope again, and found three pounds in it. I had never had so much money in my life before.

I thought of buying something decent to read. I wondered how many weeks' fares it would pay to the school over the mountain. I wondered if I could use it somehow to impress the Williamses, and make them sorry they had laughed at me. I thought of my father, at home in London, with only my aunt to talk to, and wondered idly what he looked like in uniform.

Then suddenly I stopped thinking idly. I went up the road to the station, and looked at the timetable. There was only one train a day down the valley, and only every other day at that. And I had just missed one, anyway. The man in the ticket office stared at me, curiously, and I knew that he knew who I was, and I couldn't expect to buy a ticket from him, and be asked no questions. So I went back down the road to the crossroads to look at the signpost. The signpost said *Oswestry, 15 miles*, and the timetable had told me there were connections with the London train from Oswestry. Fifteen miles. I looked at my worn, thin shoes. They wouldn't make it. I walked back up the street to the general shop, and bought a pair of boots; good tough ones, which laced up high, and had heavy studs in the soles. They cost thirty shillings, with a spare pair of laces.

'Shall I wrap them up for you?' the shopkeeper asked.

'No, thank you, I'm going to wear them right away.'

'You shouldn't do that, boy.'

'Why not?'

'You should put Dubbin on them first. If you Dubbin them well, now, when they have never been wet, they will be nicely waterproof for months. Good thing, that is.'

'I don't think I can afford Dubbin,' I said dubiously, looking at my change.

'Mrs Williams-on-the-hill's London boy, isn't it?'

'Yes.'

'Well, now, Mrs Williams is a good friend of mine. You will find a tin of Dubbin over there, on the shelf under the counter, and an old rag with it. Off with you now.'

I sat behind the counter for about half an hour, smearing Dubbin into the boots, and rubbing them up to a nice shine. The shopkeeper didn't think much of the shine I got at first, so I went back and tried again. Then he let me put them on.

I liked him. And I didn't find his being Welsh a burden to me, not now. Straightening up from lacing the boots I said to him, 'Boro da!' He smiled at me, and answered incomprehensibly.

I set off. I had no idea at all how long it would take me to walk fifteen miles, for I had never done anything like it. I must have been on bus rides as long as that, but I couldn't even remember how long the bus took. I tried to work it out from the cross-country runs we had done at school, but we did those at a trot, and on the flat, and it was pavement most of the way, and anyway, I wasn't much good at it. I gave up trying to work it out, and just walked.

Outside the village I met the baker's van, and I bought a brown bap from him, and stuffed it in my pocket. It wasn't raining that day, for once. I looked up over the river, and the roofs of the toy-town houses to the Williams farm. From a good three miles away I could see the white sheep clustered in the dipping field, and the expanse of hillside devoid of white specks above it. I remembered Evan giving me money for the stamp, and Mrs Williams' warm new-made bread. I felt quite friendly towards them.

There was nobody else on the road. It twisted a good deal, winding down the valley, with the stream beside it all the way. Every mile or so there was a farm gate. The valley widened out as it descended. Over the other side the railway to the quarry scored a straight line on the lower slopes of the hillside, and once I saw a string of trucks go down, and heard them rattle, the rattle rebounding in the valley all the way.

When the sun stood high in the sky, and my new boots began to feel hot and heavy, I stopped and lay down in the hedgerow, and ate my bap. Then I climbed a gate and wandered across the field, and drank from the stream in my cupped hands. Vaguely I remembered an Old Testament story about soldiers drinking from their hands; but I couldn't remember whether the soldiers who drank with cupped hands were chosen, or rejected. I went back to the road.

It didn't take me so terribly long to reach Oswestry. I got there in the late afternoon. I found the railway station, and bought a ticket to London.

I ate horrible cheese sandwiches from the station buffet for tea, and waited for the train to leave. It left an hour and a half late, and struggled across England in the murky darkness, stopping every few miles, or so it seemed to me, as I drowsed in my seat. We got into Paddington very early in the morning, just at the first light. Shaking sleep from my eyes, stretching and yawning, I walked out into the streets.

There were a lot of people about, for such an early hour. A lot of them were wearing siren-suits, and tin hats, with letters painted on them, in white. Otherwise London looked the same, her usual grimy old self.

I caught a bus to go home. I sat on the upper deck, looking at the streets. In two places on the way I saw collapsed buildings, lying in a heap of rubble behind some hoardings. The wood of the hoarding looked new, still raw and clean. It carried posters. I remember one of them said, 'A grand use for stale bread!' And I shuddered, and felt a brief twinge of regret for Mrs Williams' kitchen, and soft Welsh talk in the suffused fragrance of new baking.

Then suddenly the bus took a wrong turn. It rattled away in the new direction, and I looked up and said to the conductress, 'Where are we going?'

'Don't ask me, mate,' she said.

'Well what's up?' I demanded. 'We're going the wrong way.'

'Haven't you heard there's a war on?' she said. 'For all I know the street ain't there no more.'

But I could see down the side turnings, and all the streets were still there. I rang the bell, and scrambled off the bus. I started to walk towards home. Everything looked the same. I wasn't surprised at that; I didn't know why it shouldn't. At the corner by the traffic lights a newspaper stall had the headlines, MORE HEAVY RAIDS 30 ENEMY AIRCRAFT SHOT DOWN.

We lived on high rising ground, with a view at the end of every street. I remember seeing haze in the air over London, where usually, between the rows of houses, one saw quite clearly the skyline of the City: spires, and the dome of St Paul's. I thought only that it was misty that morning. Then I rounded the corner, and turned down my own street.

Right across the street, halfway down, was a barricade made of kitchen chairs, and a couple of oil drums with string rigged across them. Propped up against the middle chair was a red board, which announced in roughly-painted white letters: DANGER UNEXPLODED BOMB.

A few doors down from the notice, my aunt's house stood, just the same. The roses in the tiny front garden were in a riot of overblown flower. The little iron gate was shut. But the stone step under the gate looked dirty; it hadn't been scrubbed down yesterday. I think that, more than the notice, told me that she wasn't there.

In a doorway, just beside the barrier, a man was leaning, half asleep. He was wearing a siren suit, and his tin hat had W painted on it. He stared at me. I was standing there, in the middle of the road, looking at the notice.

'What do you think you're doing?' he said.

'Going home.'

'Where's home, sonny?' In spite of his weariness, he was taking an interest in me.

'Down there.'

'Sorry, no go. Not till the bomb unit come and debug the bomb. There's nobody there, anyway.'

'I don't see a bomb,' I said, sullenly. I was bewildered, resentful, the way one is when something has been going on one doesn't know about.

'It's in the back gardens, down there.'

'Where have they gone?'

'Who?'

'All the people in these houses.'

'Oh, to stay with relations I suppose. There's a rest centre in the High Street. If they haven't anywhere else to go, they'll be there.'

'Can't I just go home, and wait for her to come back?' I asked. 'And my Dad's due home, too. What will he do?'

'Look, son,' he said, still wearily, but with an edge on his voice. 'There's a bloody great bomb down there, that's maybe going up any minute. You go across that barricade and you'll maybe set it off; well, you would have asked for it, wouldn't you, so never mind what would happen to you; but you'd wreck a whole street full of houses, and maybe kill someone else who hadn't asked for nothing. See? Now get moving.'

But I just stood there. I was tired, and suddenly, I suppose, afraid. I must have looked it, too.

'I wonder what you're doing here, anyway,' he said. 'You shouldn't be here at all.' Startled, I stared at him, guiltily. 'They should have sent you away,' he said.

From behind me came footsteps, in clattering boots. His relief warden had arrived. As they greeted each other, and began to talk, I turned and wandered away, going idly down the street. On the doorsteps the milk bottles were standing, and as I passed number 40 a woman opened the door, and stooped, and took hers in. Her windows were all criss-crossed with brown sticky paper, and draped in white damask netting. A newsboy on a bicycle came towards me, stopping to push papers through the letterboxes. Down at the corner a policeman appeared wearing a soldier's tin hat, instead of a familiar helmet. Beyond him was a small hut, with walls made of sandbags, and a fire burning in a bucket full of holes at the doorway. It had a notice on it, 'Warden's Post'. Beyond that again, I could see a long, low, windowless brick thing, standing in the middle of Station Road. That had S painted on it, in shiny grey paint. 'S?' I thought. 'Oh, Shelter, I suppose.'

Suddenly, as though I had been dreaming before, I saw how different it all was, how everything had changed. Here and there houses I had known all my life had crumbled away, fallen in a heap into their own basements, leaving a lost-tooth gap in the skyline, and all around me the adults were changed; all with tired faces, all busy, walking by me. The warden standing warming his hands at the brazier was only the school caretaker, wearing different clothes. He looked at me, but did not see me, or did not seem to.

Then suddenly I thrilled with excitement, felt it tingling the length of my spine. I was free. Nobody was going to look after me; nobody was going to worry, or plan for me, or make me eat on time, or delouse me, or keep me safe from harm. They were all wrapped up in something else; they were all having the war. Well, I was going to have a war too; and my war was going to be just like theirs, staying in London, staying put.

I was going to manage on my own till my Dad came home.

3

Over breakfast in Marco's I told most of this tale to the girl. She listened willingly enough. It was nearly a week later by then, and I had managed on my own all that time. I didn't tell her how I had done it, because I wanted to make sure she would stay with me; I had been pretty lonely. She seemed willing enough about that too.

When she had at last had enough of Marco's coffee, we wandered out again, and strolled down to the Embankment, and walked along by the river. As we passed each lamp-post on the wall, those lamp-posts with sleek Dolphins wound around the bases, she patted the Dolphin's nose. She smiled absently as she did it.

'I like them too,' I said. She had rather long hair, dark, very straight, and she kept it tucked behind her ears, but a strand kept slipping free, and falling across her face, and then she tossed her head to get rid of it. A fierce little gesture, like a horse – she should have stamped her foot at the same time – but then her face appearing from behind the errant hair wasn't fierce at all.

'What shall we do now?' she said.

'Oh, we have time to spend. What would you like to do?'

'I'd like to go and buy some blankets. I was *very* cold on that platform last night.'

'We can't *buy* them.'

'I told you, I've got plenty of money. Lots and lots.'

'However much you've got, you'll need it in the end, for food and things. You'd better hang on to it.'

'*We'd* better, you mean. We're going to stick together, aren't we?'

'If you like,' I said loftily, pretending I was doing her a favour. 'But before I take any of your money,

I think you ought to tell me how you got it, and why you ran away, and all about you.'

'You let me pay for breakfast without asking,' she said.

I was stung. 'All right, don't tell me,' I said. 'I don't need you, I'm all right by myself. Hope you make out all right. Cheerio.'

She looked frightened again, as she had when she first saw me following her. 'I'll tell you, Bill, only don't go off and leave me,' she said. 'Please.'

We sat down on a bench, under the plane trees, a little way down from Cleopatra's Needle. 'I was on that ship,' she said.

'What ship?'

'The one that was torpedoed.'

'What one that was . . . ?'

'Goodness, don't you read the papers?'

'I haven't had money to throw around on papers,' I said.

'Well, you know lots of children were being sent to Canada, and one of the shiploads of them was torpedoed in the middle of the Atlantic . . .'

'You were on that? What was it like?'

'Not so much fun as it sounds. It was only a sort of thump, and the alarm bell ringing. Then we all went up on deck, and stood in rows, just like they'd showed us in port, and then we climbed down ladders into lifeboats, and they rowed us across to the other ships that were with us, destroyers and things. Then the ships took us back to Southampton.'

'So you ran away because you didn't want to go on another ship?'

'Well, not exactly.'

'Were you afraid?'

'No, no, it wasn't that.' (I wished it had been, somehow.) 'It was just that most of the others went home; their parents took them home again for a few days, until the next ship went, and mine didn't want to see me again, so I was left with a few others in this horrid hostel place, and I didn't like it, so I walked out.'

'Why didn't they want to see you again?' I asked.

She flinched. 'My father rang up, and said, "Now then, my girl, I'm sure you don't want to put your mother through all that performance again, do you?" So then I couldn't very well say yes, yes I did, could I?'

'What performance?' I asked, deeply puzzled by her account.

'You aren't exactly quick on the uptake, are you?' she said. 'Saying goodbye, of course.'

'What about the money?' I said, trying to change the subject a bit.

'It was for Canada. You aren't allowed to send money over there, so it was for looking after me there for quite a time.'

'Are you going to find them?'

'Mummy and Daddy you mean? Can't. Daddy's in the army, and might be anywhere, and when I got here, last night, there wasn't anyone here, either. I don't know where they are.'

'Did you live in London then?'

'No. It was my aunt's house. I thought my mother would be with my aunt. I haven't been to London for ages and ages, and as soon as we've found some blankets, I want to go and see Big Ben, and Nelson's column. Do you know the way?'

'Of *course* I do!' I laughed. 'Let's go now.'

'Blankets first,' she said, firmly.

'Are you sure the money is yours, all right for you to spend?'

'Quite sure. You're a bit fussed about money, aren't you? Are you poor?'

'No,' I said, taken aback. 'No, I don't think so. My aunt was always on about money, but we always had enough of things, and warm clothes, and Dad bought my uniform for me when I won a place at Grammar school.'

'I'm sorry,' she said, looking a little pink. 'My mother said only poor people talk about money. Anyway, they aren't poor. They wouldn't miss it if I spent the whole fifty pounds on blankets.'

'*Fifty pounds?*' I said. '*Fifty pounds?*'

'How long will it last us,' she asked, 'if we're careful with it?'

'Oh, for ever, I should think,' I said. 'Just about for ever!' That great feeling of freedom swept over me again.

'Oh, ripping!' she said, grinning at me. 'That should be long enough. The war won't last for ever, will it, Bill?'

'Come on,' I said, starting to run away, along the pavement by the river. 'Come on!'

Later we sat in St James's Park, on the grass beside the lake. There was barbed-wire all over the Horse Guards parade, and the soldiers on guard there were in khaki; but we had been to Trafalgar Square, and Whitehall. There were wardens' posts and shelters covered in sandbags set up round the edge of the park, but the middle was the same as it used to be. We were eating lunch; sandwiches, and mugs of hot tea, bought from a W.V.S. canteen in a lorry parked in the Mall. There was some sort of fire-fighting exercise going on, and people marked A.F.S. were swarming over from Green Park, and the canteen was for them really, but they didn't mind serving us. They were hearty women in green overcoats, very cheerful.

While we were sitting there an air-raid warning sounded; a horrible wailing noise, running up and down the scale.

'What's that?' cried Julie, jumping up. 'Oh, what do we have to do?'

'Have some more beef sandwich!' I yelled at her, raising my voice above the din.

'Where are the shelters, Bill? Oh, come on, run!' she said.

'They're too far. Right at the edge of the park,' I said. 'We'll be all right here.'

People around us were picking themselves up, and walking away. 'We don't want to be seen, or they'll tell us to take cover,' I said. 'Let's go over there.' I led the way into a clump of rhododendrons, and we lay down on the leaf mould beneath the branches, out of sight. I lay on my back, munching, and looking at a patch of sky framed by the dark leaves overhead. Then I turned my head, and looked at her. She was very white; so pale that a few faint freckles across her nose and cheeks showed up for the first time.

'It's all right,' I said. 'They blow a whistle for immediate danger, in lots of factories and offices. We'd probably hear it.'

'Oh,' she said, letting out a long breath, 'I didn't know.' Then we heard a droning noise above us. There was a line of white across our patch of sky. We could see planes up there, wheeling and diving, soaring, and chalking crazy scribbled loops on the sky. If they were shooting at each other the noise was drowned by the Ack-ack guns which opened up all around us, stuttering angrily at the sky. Then the fight moved away beyond Victoria. The guns were quiet. We lay there still, and looked at the empty park. It was full of birds: water birds, tree birds. They did not take cover, nor even flutter at the sound of guns. At last the all-clear sounded, one smooth note, and gradually people reappeared, and we got up, and went out of the park to see Big Ben. The blankets we had bought that morning were in a new canvas rucksack over my shoulder.

'I wonder what they're like close to?' she said, half to herself.

'What?'

'Those planes we were watching.'

'I'll show you,' I said. We walked across the top of Whitehall, just beside King Charles, waiting for the traffic. Lots of the passing cars were sploshed with brown and green paint, for camouflage, and one even had a mattress strapped across the roof, to absorb bullets. On the other side of the street was a little toyshop, selling mostly those horribly painted soldiers which people buy as souvenirs. But it had planes there too. There weren't many toys around in the war, and most of them were horrid, but there were those tiny planes, exact little models, made of some super shiny metal that looked just like aluminium, though I suppose it can't really have been, when people were being asked to give up their saucepans for the war effort. We looked into the windows for a bit, and I told her the names of all the different planes.

Then I dug into my pockets, and found my very last sixpence, all that I had left of the money my father sent me, and I slipped inside, and bought one of the Spitfires. I felt a bit silly when I got out onto the pavement again, so I thrust my hands into my pockets, and sauntered off down the street, with Julie trotting beside me. 'Just wanted a closer look,' I said, lightly.

'For an awful moment I thought you were trying to shake me off,' she said.

'No,' I said, suddenly serious. 'No, I won't do that, I promise you. We might as well stick together. And girls really shouldn't go around all by themselves. I think I'll look after you.'

'Thanks, Bill,' she said. 'You're a brick.'

I think it was because I had half expected her to say that anyway she had the money, that I thought this remark so splendid. I felt solid, and brick-like all the way down Whitehall.

We looked at Big Ben from Westminster Bridge, and then from Parliament Square. We heard it strike two. Then we wandered around the Abbey, giggling at the dramatic monuments to white marble gentlemen who seemed so pleased with themselves, although they were dead.

Outside again we walked past the statue of Cromwell; beyond it the road was cordoned off. Two men were sweeping the pavement; it was scattered across with lumps of stone, and shattered glass. As we rounded the corner of Westminster Hall we saw what it was. Half the great east window of the hall had been blown out, and was lying across the pavement around the foot of Richard Coeur de Lion, and his bronze horse, I remember how black the yawning gap in the tracery looked. It brought things home to me, that. Seeing ugly old shops and shabby houses knocked apart had not seemed so appalling as seeing the wreckage of that lovely patterned stone.

'Bloody swine!' I muttered.

'How awful,' she said, very softly. We stood looking for a minute. I remember that the fragments of stone were grey where they had been exposed to the grimy London air, and creamy yellow where they had been broken across. Splinters of glass lay among them, sparkling in pale sunlight. I looked sideways at Julie. Her face looked very still and quiet. Then suddenly, as she raised her head to toss away her hair, the gloom on her countenance lightened, till she almost laughed.

'Oh, look, Bill, look!' she said, pointing to the Lionheart, riding above us. Proudly, above his head, pointing skywards, he held his great longsword; but the sword was bent. At first glance it made the great horseman look comic; both of us were laughing aloud. But then, as we let laughter die away we saw that it also made him look resolute, and turned the cheap heroics of his gesture into a battered defiance that would not be overcome.

The sweeper nearest us raised his head and, nodding towards the statue, said to us:

'Don't seem to bother '*im*, do it?'

'Will they be able to mend the window?' Julie asked him.

'Stones is easier to mend than bones,' he told her. 'Mind you gets tucked up safely at night, young miss.'

We wandered on. 'Now we've got a rucksack to put things in,' I said thoughtfully, there are a lot of things from home I wish I had.'

'What sort of things?'

'My penknife, for a start. And my torch. And something to read when I can't get to sleep in those shelters. And I'd very much like a shave.'

'*Shave?*' she said, incredulous. 'You don't need to shave!'

'I jolly well do! About once a week or so.'

'Well, I can't see any beard on you.' She stared at my chin.

I raised my hand instinctively, and stroked the soft absurd pale down that grew there. She laughed again.

'Really, Bill, you don't need to shave *that* off! That's not a beard!'

'It makes me feel a fool,' I said, sourly.

'Oh. Oh, I'm sorry. Well, let's go back to your house.'

'I suppose I really ought to go and see if my aunt's there again now,' I said. I hadn't really meant to go back right away. I felt very reluctant, as though something nasty would happen if I saw anyone I knew, though I hadn't the sense to work out why I felt like that. Stands out a mile to me, looking back, but as Julie said, I wasn't very quick on the uptake. After all, I was only fifteen.

We went home on an Underground train. It was very smelly down there, because of all the night shelters. They left their stink behind them. The barricade was still across the road. The doorstep was even more dirty, and all the windows looked dead; I don't know how it is that one can see from the glass, as one can in human eyes, when there's nobody at home, but it's true. We didn't walk straight up the street to be caught and warned off by the warden, but slipped round the little lane that led between the small gardens at the back. That too had a notice, UNEXPLODED BOMB, propped up against an old oil can, but we just walked past it.

I opened the gate at the end of our garden, and we went down the path. It looked different: the leaves were all golden yellow on the apple tree, and the grass had grown long, and was jewelled with dew, even then, in the afternoon. At the end of the garden, next to the house, was a deep pit, about six feet wide, into which the windows of the basement looked. It had stone steps into it, which led to the back door. And lying in this sunk place, lodged against the kitchen windowsill on one side, and against my aunt's parsley and mint patch on the other, was the bomb. Its nose-cone was on the windowsill, poking through a broken pane, and its finned tail was on the herb bed. We stared at it, fascinated. Looking up I saw broken branches in the apple tree, and looking down I saw a long scuffed mark on the lawn.

'Look, Julie,' I said, excited. 'It fell into the tree, and that must have broken its fall a bit, and turned it sideways, so that it slithered along the lawn, instead of falling on its nose, and that's why it didn't go off. It just slipped along there, and stuck.' Indeed, the scuff marks and scratches on its grey sides were already bright with new rust and where the leaky gutter spilled over it it had grown a streak of livid green algae, absurdly, as though it meant just to stay there, and weather into the surround-ings like a fallen tree.

'I don't like it,' she said. 'Let's go.'

I think I would have said it if she hadn't, but now she had I felt different. 'No,' I said. 'I want my things.'

Her face whitened, visibly, as I watched. 'But we'd have to go right under it!' she said.

'Cowardy, cowardy, custard!' I said, to make myself feel brave.

'Are you really going to?' she asked.

'Yes,' I said, 'Really.'

'Well, if you are, I'm coming too,' she said, firmly, taking a tight hold of my hand, and marching me towards it.

So we went. We walked down the steps, and across the narrow yard, stooping under the bomb, past it, and getting to the door. I slipped my hand round the doorpost, and found the key, as always, wedged between the doorpost and the wall, where the fit was bad. I turned it in the lock, and let us in.

It was dark. The bomb blocked out a lot of the light. Its nasty snout was nearly resting on the draining board beside the sink. Broken glass from the window lay across the floor, and dust lay thick on the table and the dresser. Julie was shivering. I heard her teeth. You know people say teeth chatter, and that's just what hers were doing. I don't know what came over me, but I looked and looked, and saw how she was, shivering, hugging herself round with her arms, her eyes looking huge and dark, and it made me feel cruel.

'I want a cup of tea,' I said. 'I'm going to shave. Make me a cup of tea.'

We both looked round the place, seeing the horror of what I had just said. There were tile cups and the teapot on the dresser; about five steps away. Then five steps back to get the kettle from the stove. Then the tap, about three inches from the surface of the bomb. Then the stove again.

'The gas!' she said, very breathlessly. 'They'll have turned off the gas! They must have turned it off, must have! It might explode,' she added in a more normal tone.

'It's an electric stove,' I said brutally. 'And the mains switch is just above it,' and full of manly strength I went off up the stairs, three at a time, to the bathroom.

I was sorry by the time I had lathered my face. I hoped she would come up and join me, but she didn't. I hoped she wouldn't set it off; I supposed she would kill me too if she did, and that made it all right to be up here, shaving. It wasn't as if I was safe. My razor blades had got rusty while I was in Wales, and the water was cold, so it took some time. Then I went and fetched my torch and penknife from my room, and some clean socks while I was at it, and a shirt, and that copy of *Kidnapped* that I had pretended to read when I was angry with my aunt. Then I went downstairs to the kitchen.

She had the tea made, cups laid on the table. The table had been dusted too. She had even found a packet of biscuits in the larder and put them out. Her own tea was poured out, and she was sitting reading one of my aunt's copies of *Picture Post*.

I stood in the, doorway, looking at her. I expected her to be triumphant, gloating; or maybe, to reproach me for my monstrous behaviour, sullen stares like the ones my aunt was so good at. Instead she looked up and grinned at me, and said, 'Come and have some tea! Look at this.'

'This' was a picture in the magazine, of St Paul's Cathedral. The heading was UNEXPLODED BOMB THREATENS ST PAUL'S. We could see a great yawning black hole in the pavement outside the south transept. Heads together, while we drank tea, we read about the bomb disposal squad, who were trying to deal with the bomb. They had dug down thirty feet before reaching it, and were still trying to defuse it when the paper went to press.

'You know,' she said, 'it's supposed to be good.'

'What is?'

'St Paul's.'

'How do you mean, good?'

'It's supposed to be good architecture. People who know think so. And I've only seen it once, when I was quite young, and I didn't like it much then. I'd like to go and see it again, just once more, while it's still there.'

'It'll still be there,' I said. 'These bomb gangs are dealing with it.'

'Bill,' she said, slowly. 'Do you know anything much about bombs?'

'Well, no, only what I've read in the papers.'

'My father used to do them in the first war. Get the fuses out, you know. It's very dangerous.'

'Well, as long as you don't give them a great knock on the nose-cone. That's what makes them go off, isn't it?'

'You've got it a bit muddled, I think,' she said, pouring out more tea. 'Some of the ones that don't go off are duds, or ordinary ones that just by some chance didn't fall on the trigger mechanism, but some of them are real time bombs, meant not to go off till someone touches them. They make a lot of trouble you see, making people leave that area, and all that. And those ones, Daddy said, are specially made to go off at the lightest touch, anywhere on them. Or even at a loud noise. Or even a change in temperature. The people who deal with them are just about the bravest people there are, Mummy says.'

'Golly,' I said. 'I should think your mother's right. O.K., we'll take a bus back to town. There's one that goes right by St Paul's, and you can take your last look.' It was a sort of delayed reaction, like the way a wave breaks, and then the backwash breaks again. I was still chatting about the bomb at St Paul's when I remembered the one behind me.

'Julie,' I said. My throat was quite dry. Very slowly I picked up my cup of tea, and gulped some. 'Julie, which sort do you think this is: the accident sort, or the time-bomb-go-off-at-any-time-sort?'

'I honestly don't know,' she said, looking up at me calmly, with dark, limpid eyes. 'I haven't a clue.'

And I made her make the tea. 'Come on,' I said. 'Let's get out of here!'

'Let's!' she said, getting up at once. Then at the door she said, 'Have you got your things?'

'Yes,' I said. 'I put them in the rucksack.' I was whispering.

'Good,' she said. 'Only I wouldn't like you to make us come back for them!' I have never closed a door so gently in my life as I closed that kitchen door behind me.

The bomb went up some time after we left. How long after I'm not sure. It wrecked the houses on either side of my aunt's, and two houses across the road, and it blew in the windows all the way down the street. Where our house had been there was nothing left but a great hole. But the apple tree, split in two right to the root, sent up a shoot the following spring, and survived. I can get my aunt to talk about it any time.

4

We sat on top of the bus, choosing a seat where someone had peeled off the new mesh netting from the windows, so that we could look out. The netting was to stop the window hurling splinters of glass at the passengers, but it made it so hard to see where one was that people pulled it off. Our window was all mucky with the glue left behind by the net. It was late afternoon, with that sort of misty haze in the air that the sun shines through softly, making no shadows.

'Bill, tell me how ever you've managed all this time,' said Julie.

'It's not so hard as you'd think,' I said.

'But you had hardly any money; have you been getting enough to eat?'

'I did have some money at first. You don't have to pay to sleep; you just go down a shelter. Nobody notices, because there are lots of people floating around on their own. And there are special places to buy food, you know, like the W.V.S. canteen where we got lunch.'

'Don't they move around a lot? How do you know you'll find them?'

'Well, there are dumps called British War Restaurants, that stay put, in church halls, and places like that. You can get a good meal there for sixpence, if you don't take pudding.'

'Did your money last until this morning?'

'No, but I earned some. It's not hard to do. I delivered newspapers for a few days, for a chap who'd lost all his delivery boys through evacuation; but then I found a better way. All the street markets are short handed; it's the old gents who are left, and some of them are trying to run their son's stall as well, and he's in the army, or some such thing. And they pay you quite well to mind the stall, and yell "Sweet Kentish plums!" at people. The best bit is, they feed you as well as pay you – you can eat all the squashed fruit and flattened buns and broken cake you can stuff into yourself. And they don't ask you any questions, either, not like the newsagent, who was always worrying about who I was and where my family were, and why I hadn't gone with all the others. I got fed up telling him fibs. But the barrow-boys aren't like that at all, they just say, "Them as asks no questions don't get told no lies".'

'Oh, Bill,' she said, eyes shining, 'What fun! Can I come too?'

I looked at her doubtfully. 'You'd stick out like a sore thumb in that posh dress,' I said. 'We'd have to get you something a bit raggedy.'

'How could we do that?' she asked.

'From the Salvation Army Mission. They got me this jacket when the weather went cold. They don't ask too much, either. The only trouble is, all their stuff's too big.' And I pulled at my jacket, to show her how far in front of my chest it buttoned up.

She laughed. 'Bill, you could get two of you in there, easily,' she said. Then she began to giggle. 'And wait till I tell Mother. *She* said this dress would do to go *anywhere*!'

'Golly, look at that!' I said. Outside the smeary window of the bus we could see a terrible sight. There was a great wide desolate stretch of blasted houses. Piles of rubble lay thickly everywhere, with splintered timbers sticking out here and there. In a few places a wall was still standing with empty windows gaping against the sky, and all crumbled and broken into strange shapes, and blackened by fire. The bus was bumping along the road, for the road surface was full of holes. People were struggling along the pavement by a narrow path swept through the rubble; the shops were fronted with boards instead of glass, and labelled 'Business as Usual' in roughly painted letters. We looked in silence.

A red-haired conductress leant over us to look out of the window. 'Gawd. I 'ope they're getting it back!' she said.

'Do we do that too?' Julie asked me.

'I don't know,' I said, shuddering.

St Paul's was still there. The hole in the pavement was there too, but it was just roped off, and the bomb had gone, for there were no notices, and the bus went right by the hole. We got off at the first stop on Ludgate Hill, and went to have a look.

'It must have been an out-of-date *Picture Post*, of course,' said Julie.

We stood at the foot of the steps, and looked at the façade.

'I still don't know, really, that I like it all that much,' she said.

'Well, but I know what they mean about it,' I told her. 'When you just remember what it looks like, you see it all columns, and a dome, and it seems very ordinary, and reminds you of the Odeon Cinema, and the town hall somewhere; but as soon as you see it again it's just a bit different, and you can see that it's right, and the people who built the town hall were just copy-cats, and got it wrong.'

'Hmm,' she said.

'It's so exact; all the shapes, and all the distances from here to there, all over it, are so exactly right.'

'Well,' she said, staring hard, 'I shall just have to remember what it's like as hard as I can, so that I can change my mind about it later, even if it's gone.'

Suddenly a voice came from behind us. 'Now, don't go saying *that*, young lady. It may never happen. Never. And what does happen is quite enough to worry about. Sufficient unto the day, you know. Or perhaps you don't. Young people today don't know their Bibles as we did.'

It was an elderly stooped old gentleman, with a stick. Very vague and benign, like all the world's grandfather.

'Sufficient unto the day are the evils thereof,' I said. I never could bear not to show off, when I knew something.

'Quite right, quite right,' he said. 'And if I may say so, it is time you young people were getting home to safety. There are raids at any time of the day, now, you know. And really the young lady looks quite tired.' He was peering at Julie now, through steel-rimmed spectacles. 'If you will allow me, I will call a taxi, and put you on it for home. Now what is your address, young man?'

I didn't see the danger till he got that far. Then I saw it, in a flash. But not quicker than Julie, who took to her heels at once, and dashed across the road, and into a narrow lane between tall buildings. I followed her, the rucksack bouncing up and down, and slapping me on the back as I ran. He waved his stick, and called after us, and just before I turned the corner, I saw him talking to a policeman and pointing his stick towards me.

Weaving through narrow streets, we ran and ran. We found ourselves in Blackfriars Bridge Road, and so on the Embankment again. Once there, we wandered along under the plane trees, saying nothing for a while.

'What would happen if we got found out?' she said at last.

'If that old geezer had reported us to someone? I suppose you would be sent to Canada, and I would be sent back to Wales.'

'Without asking us what we wanted at all?'

'Well, they didn't ask us the first time, did they?'

'We mustn't get found out,' she said fiercely. 'We mustn't let it happen.'

'No,' I said. 'We won't.'

She didn't say why we mustn't. I didn't ask.

It was getting dark as we walked. The lampposts' empty extinguished cages were outlined against the purple sky. A tug going up-river, a dim smudge of dark on the shiny water, hooted softly. The cars along the Embankment drove slowly, with deeply-hooded lights. The white lines painted along their running boards were all that we could see; they looked like white worms passing us. A tram clattered by, lurching along its faintly-shining rails. Somewhere on the South Bank search-lights opened up, long sweeping fingers groping in the sky. We turned from the river, and went up to the Strand – itself like a river, with two churches for islands – to take cover once more in the Aldwych Underground Station. From all the streets around, in all directions, processions of people were coming too, carrying their bedding, trailing tired children by the hand.

We looked upwards for a last glance at the sky. The stars were all there, shining in a mercilessly clear darkness, and soon the moon would be up, with no clouds to quench her, pouring clear silver on river, on domes, on spires, lighting every target in the city. We went down into the depths.

I remember how good it felt not to be on my own. To have someone to talk to, instead of lying as a lonely island outside all the circles of talk around me. We were lucky that night, and got a place on the platform. We lay down with the rucksack acting as a shared pillow, each rolled up in a new soft blanket. Other people came and lay all around us, till we were packed like sardines in a tin. On the curving tiles above us a poster exhorted the men to leave the space for women and children. 'The trains must run', it said. But they had stopped all trains on the Aldwych extension now. As the platform filled up people got down between the rails, and spread out their sleeping things there. Then a shelter warden appeared. He had a bundle of hammocks. He looked around, and caught my eye.

'Give us a hand, son?' I got up. Julie sat up too.

'These here 'ammocks is for the kids,' he said. 'We gotta string 'em up along there,' and he pointed to the rails. Down we went, moving people up to make some space. Grumbling a little, they edged along, far into the tunnel at the end of the platform. We tied one end of the short hammocks to the rail nearest the platform, and the other to the high-power rail. The warden and I tied them up, and Julie and a few others lifted kids out of the crush on the platform and tucked them up, swinging between the rails. At last all the hammocks were occupied, and we scrambled back, stepping over prostrate bodies, to our own places.

Somewhere on the down platform a sing-song had started up. Gusts of laughter boomed down the tunnel at us. Nearby a baby cried, until its mother lifted herself up wearily to sit leaning against the wall, giving it the breast. Beside us a large fat woman in a tight shiny black dress was handing out doughnuts from a paper bag to all her kids. She handed them to us too, without a word.

'Thank you,' said Julie. 'But . . .'

'Go on, love, treat yourself,' said the woman. We did. I remembered I had a book in the rucksack, but by now Julie was asleep on it. I needed the lavatory. There was a row of empty fire buckets at the end of the platform, but I remembered that there were real lavatories in the ticket hall upstairs. Carefully, quietly, I got up, and moved along the sleeping rows towards the exit. All the corridors leading to the platform were as thickly crowded as the platform itself. People who had found no room to stretch out were sitting on their bundles, swaying with sleepiness. A slumped form occupied nearly every step of the frozen escalators, and my trek up to the top would wake at least a hundred sleepers. Groaning, I went back to the fire buckets.

When I got back to my place, Julie was awake, looking round. 'It's O.K. I'm here,' I said. She laid her head back on the rucksack. When I rested my own head beside her I could feel the patch of warmth she had made on the canvas. And something in my back trouser pocket jabbed into me. It was the Spitfire.

'Julie,' I whispered.

'Mmm?'

'I've got a present for you. Here.' As she reached out for it in its twist of tissue paper, I saw that she was wearing a silver chain bracelet, with a disc on it, like the ones you see on dog-collars.

'For me?' she said.

'What sort is it?' I asked her. 'Do you remember?'

'A Spitfire,' she said. 'Thank you, Bill.'

'What's this?' I asked, taking the disc on her bracelet into my fingers.

'My identity disc, with my number on. Haven't you got one?'

'I've got a number, but I keep it in my head.' And yet, now, after all these years I can only remember my number with an effort, but I remember hers easily. It was ZKDN/74/8. She slipped off to sleep again with the little plane held in her hand.

Some while later there was a dull thump. I felt the ground beneath me tremble for a second, and the exit sign, hanging over our heads, rattled briefly on its wires. All around us heads were raised from the platform.

'Other side of the river,' said someone.

'By the Shot Tower,' another voice agreed. Two more bumps came quickly, one after another. 'Nearer,' people murmured, 'much nearer.'

'Safe here, though, ducks,' said the doughnut woman, 'Not to worry.' Heads were lowered to rest again.

Then I too fell asleep.

In the morning we bought tea from a trolley brought round by the shelter wardens; we waited for the people nearer the exits to go so that the crowd was not too pressing, and then we packed our rucksack, Julie lifted it onto my back, and we made our way up to the open air, and went to have breakfast at Marco's.

And that's how we managed together.

We decided straight away that we would go on working the street markets, in spite of the wad of notes rolled up in the bottom of the rucksack. After all, when that was gone there would be nothing we could do but go and give ourselves up to some adult authority. And working gave us something with which to fill our days. When we weren't working we walked a lot, endlessly round and round, covering London from the Tower to Hyde Park, over and over as the days went by. I still know London like the back of my hand, better than a taxi-driver sometimes; I'll bet she does too. When it rained we rode about on buses.

We weren't the only ones. There were hordes of other children, playing around in the streets. As before, a lot of parents had brought their children home after a week or two, and the schools were all closed so they roamed the streets. We played football, and even tag and hopscotch with them in the side streets, when we got tired of the coster-mongers' stalls. Some of them sold black-market sweets to us, too.

We saw London getting knocked apart. We knew where there was ruin, and we knew that it wasn't all in the papers. We saw a lot of terrible things. But the strangest thing, in a way, was the way things were the same. It sounds silly to say that the oddest thing was that the leaves turned gold, and fell off, while Hitler's bombers filled the sky; of course they would, and they did. But in all that disruption, in the midst of so much destruction, when everyone's life was changed, and we were alone, standing on our own feet for the first time, looking after ourselves, familiar things seemed as exotic and unlikely as hothouse flowers.

People were different then, too. They were tired, nearly all of them, from having so little sleep, from being woken every night, from being frightened. But they were friendly. They talked to each other on buses, in the streets, in the shelters. At first we were alarmed when people spoke to us; we thought they were all going to jump on us, and report us to someone (Heaven knows whom), for being on our own. But we soon stopped feeling like that. They weren't in that mood, somehow.

'Where's your mum 'n dad?' someone asked us one night, in a big street shelter near Hyde Park.

'I don't know,' I said.

'Cheer up, son,' she said. 'Things happen. Perhaps they'll turn up.'

I realized she thought I meant they were bombed. I felt a bit ashamed then, as though I had told a mean sort of lie.

'Are you all right?' she was asking. 'Got food and money? Know where to go?'

'Thank you,' I said. 'But yes, thanks, we're all right.'

'That's plucky,' she said. 'As long as we've got enough like you.'

In some of the shelters people had sing-songs, drank beer, even danced. An old man played the accordion, and everyone sang, 'Oh, Johnnie, oh Johnnie, how you can love!' and 'We'll hang out the washing on the Siegfried Line' and 'Wish me luck as you wave me goodbye!' That was fun, but it went on so late we felt very limp the next day, so the following night we went somewhere else, to get some sleep.

Then there were always some people who told

endless jokes, raising a laugh somehow. After all this time I can still remember a toothless old man saying, 'Talk about laugh! She paid into the insurance for years to be buried proper, and it took them three days to dig her out!' They did laugh, too.

We saw men digging. They had black tin hats, with R painted on them for rescue. They were always dirty, covered with powdered plaster and mud. We would see them scrambling on piles of debris, or from the top of the bus glimpse them down a hole in the rubble, and always there would be a stretcher party standing by, and an ambulance parked somewhere near.

I remember us working a stall once, selling oranges. It had been trundled onto a pile of rubble at a street corner, and it boasted a huge notice saying, OUR ORANGES HAVE COME THROUGH MUSSO'S LAKE! They sold well, too. There was an air-raid going on, but we weren't taking much notice, and neither was anyone else near us. They happened too often. They lasted too long. One just got tired of it, just couldn't react for every one. So there we were selling oranges, brought past Mussolini's destroyers, and eaten under Hitler's Luftwaffe.

Suddenly there was a terrible racket a little way off; sirens, and fire-bells, and a roar of flame so fierce we could hear it where we stood. The sky over towards St Paul's filled with billowing smoke, and then the underside of the black smoke-cloud lit up a lurid yellow. Cinders the size of saucers fell around us. And out of the doorway of the Paradise Buildings, opposite our stall, a bloke came running like a maniac. He had a helmet on, and an Auxiliary Fire Service jacket, which he was still buttoning as he ran, and he was wearing his pyjama trousers. Poor devil must have been snatching a bit of sleep. He was stout, I remember, and a large triangle of hairy belly showed through where the pyjamas tied. Panting for breath he ran off towards the fire.

'Go on Charlie!' cried a delighted crowd of onlookers.

'Had enough shut-eye?'

Cupping his hands to his mouth the barrow boy beside us bellowed after him, 'Where's your trousers?'

He disappeared into the foul-smelling wall of smoke at the far end of the street. Fire-fighting must take guts at the best of times, but the fires caused by incendiary bombs were like acres of hell itself. And he was such an ordinary sort of bloke, fat and hairy, and a bit red in the face . . .

'You know what, Bill,' said Julie beside me. 'His pyjamas are like the Lionheart's sword.'

Then there was Little Bert. Big Bert and Little Bert kept a stall in Leather Lane market. Big Bert wasn't very big, but he was Little Bert's dad. He was too old to go into the army, and Little Bert was too young. They had a stall that sold bits and pieces, plugs, coils of wire, things for making crystal sets, simple wireless receivers, light bulbs, all that sort of thing.

'Wireless. That's a larf,' Big Bert used to say, showing us the back of one. We often worked beside them, taking a turn at selling fruit and veg for an enormous woman called Ma Johnson, so that she could 'Go and 'ava cuppa'.

'You know, Bill,' said Julie. 'I'm awfully ignorant. Really. I never knew they sold tea in pubs.' I laughed at her till I could hardly stand straight, I got such a stitch.

'Oh, yes, Julie, you are!' I told her.

'Well, no need to rub it in!' she said, crossly.

Anyway, one day when we were keeping Ma Johnson's stall a bomb fell right in front of us. Just like that. No siren had sounded, and what with the traffic down in Holborn I hadn't even heard the plane. It was an incendiary, and it came with a swish and a thump, and immediately a loud hissing noise, and flame began to come out of a nozzle on the top. There was a lot of noise, people diving into doorways, running, women screaming . . . and then Little Bert walked right up to it, and picked it up. It was quite a weight, so he had to hold it tight to his chest, and duck his head sideways a bit, out of the way of the jet of flame. The jet of flame was acting like a firework, getting taller and louder, working up to something.

'Oh, Bert!' cried Julie, and she flung herself into my arms, and buried her face in my jacket. Bert looked around, and his eye caught a great big water tank that stood on the street corner. It was a reserve supply for fire-fighting. They kept it topped up, using a hydrant from the pavement in case the mains supply got cut off in a raid. Bert walked over to it, staggering a bit under the weight of the thing, and people shrank away on either side as he carried it past them. He just heaved it over the top, into the water tank. There was a big splash, soaking him from top to toe, and a brief sizzle . . . and that was it.

We all stood there, dazed, staring at him. There

was so little sign of what had just happened that some newly-arrived shoppers began to get angry and shout at us because we weren't jumping to serve them.

'Cor lumme, son!' yelled Big Bert. 'Do us a favour, will yer? Gimme time to look away next time!'

Little Bert was looking a bit blank, and vaguely brushing at his clothes, to get rid of the wet. A very angry woman was yelling, 'You gonna sell me this bulb, or ain't yer?' at Big Bert.

'I'm *not*,' said Big Bert. 'Come and have a snifter, son, and get yerself dry.'

'Well, what do you want me to do with it, then?' bawled the woman, waving her thirty-watter under Big Bert's nose.

'Stuff it up yer jumper!' he said, going off down the road with his arm round Little Bert's damp shoulder. Someone started singing 'For he's a jolly good fellow!' and the whole lane joined in, stamping their feet and clapping. Little Bert went very red. Then, as soon as they rounded the corner everyone was talking at once, 'Did you see that? Nasty great thing . . . Could have killed someone . . . Cool as cucumber, 'e was . . .'

The woman beside us put the light bulb into her

shopping bag, and quick as a flash Julie was round behind Bert's stall, saying, 'That'll be a tanner, please, Mum. Can't let her get away with it,' she muttered to me.

Some men came and fished the bomb out of the tank, and put it on a lorry, and drove it away. We kept the two Berts' stall all day, while they celebrated somewhere. We had even half packed-up for them by the time they came back. They invited us to supper with them.

Mrs Big Bert opened the door, and they pushed us in ahead of them, saying, 'Guess what happened to our Bert, Ma!'

Ma listened, unwrapping fish and chips, and tipping it onto plates as she did so, saying, 'Gawd. Oh Gawd,' every now and then as the story unfolded. She sent her small girl down the road to get more fish and chips for us, and we had a good time with them that evening.

In fact we had a good time all the time, all through those days. Julie made me laugh a lot, and I kept making her laugh too, without quite meaning to; it just happened. Laughter seemed suddenly to blow up around us, like the swirling wind-borne leaves. It caught other people too; they smiled at us, suddenly, when they saw us, for no reason at all. Yet all around us death and ruin rained out of the sky. We saw it everywhere, and we were afraid like everybody else, and yet it cast no shadow in our hearts.

Every autumn takes me back to it now. Every year, when the light softens, and the mists come blurring the edges, and the colours glow and fade, I am back there again, walking the London streets. When the wind lifts the leaves along the Embankment I can even imagine I see her, in an old brown mackintosh seven sizes too big, which we got from the Salvation Army Mission.

'Ugh! Ugh, Bill, it stinks here! Why does it stink?'

The roadsweeper looked up, and said, 'Bomb broke the outfall from the main sewer, that's why.'

The next day, I remember, it stank of disinfectant.

We got so used to seeing houses collapsed in piles of rubble halfway across the street we took no more notice of them than of lamp-posts. Yet many of the sights we walked past without a second glance stand out clearly now in my mind's eye. When the roofs were blown off the houses one could see daylight falling through into the upstairs rooms; one could see the pattern of the wallpaper on the inside walls up there. Shrapnel made shallow, conical holes in the pavement and walls, with cracks running outwards from them. Often the whole of a street, from side to side, would be covered with a light layer of broken bits and pieces, as though it had fallen like hailstones from a great height. And once we walked down a street with shops on either side, and there was a big window broken, knocked inwards most of it, but a little glass across the street. And then a little way further down, there was another, on the other side, and all the windows between were all right. Then on our own side again, another window gone, about fifteen yards further down, and then on the other side, and so on like that all down the street. At the bottom of the street was a great yawning bomb crater; the blast had ricocheted, zigzag down the road.

I suppose we must have known, somewhere down inside, that we ourselves might get hurt. We can't really have believed that it could go on for ever, all that freedom, that we could go drifting through the city for ever, like birds. We must have known there would be trouble coming. But I don't remember knowing. I remember running, playing hide-and-seek in St James's Park, eating at Marco's and other places, sleeping in shelters, selling oranges, and laughing.

And when trouble came, I hardly recognized it at first, and wasn't on my guard at all.

It came with a young man in a brown tweed jacket, who came and sat beside us at the foot of the escalator at the Strand, when we were settling down for the night. Of course, I should have known it was odd; there were not many new faces down there, and almost no young men at all. He kept looking sideways at us, as we got rolled into our blankets, and got more or less comfortable. I picked up my copy of *Kidnapped*, to read while I fell asleep.

'You're nice and cosy for the night,' said the young man to us, suddenly. 'But what do you do all day?'

'We manage,' said Julie, curtly.

'Not bored at all?' he asked, smiling.

'No,' she said, and turning her back on him, lay down, and pulled the blanket over her head.

'What school were you at, before the war?' he said to me.

I told him.

'Grammar school?' he said. 'And you look almost a young man. You must have been in the sixth form.'

'I would have been, by now,' I told him. 'I was going to try for a scholarship to university.'

'That's too good a chance to miss,' he said eagerly. 'Look, I'm a schoolmaster . . .' (I should have known. One look at that tweedy jacket should have told me.) '. . . and I and some others are back in London, looking for boys to teach. You shouldn't be running wild on the streets. We have a cellar, and some desks. We'll keep you going, and find someone to coach you for those exams. Your sister can come along too, till the girls' school gets going again. Now just give me your names, and your address, and I'll go and see your parents about it.'

Julie sat up, wide-eyed.

'No,' I said, reaching for the rucksack with one hand. The worst of it was, I liked the snooping rotter in a sort of way, and he was reminding me about that scholarship . . .

'Come on now, old chap,' he said, 'be reasonable.'

'I'm over fourteen,' I said. 'You can't make me go back to school.'

'If you were at a Grammar school, your father signed you up for longer, I'm sure,' he said, getting curt and angry now. 'And your sister *is* under leaving age. Come on now, your name and address.'

By this time we had got our hands on all our possessions, and we just dashed for the escalator, and made a run for it.

'Come BACK!' he bellowed, making everyone look around at us, and he started after us, yelling all the way. 'It's no good running! You can't go out with a raid on! We've got someone in every shelter for miles, do you hear?' He began to get short of breath, and his shouting had gaps in it. 'We . . . are . . . looking . . . every night . . . in all the shelters . . . one of us . . . will find you . . . and on the streets . . . You'll have to tell someone, sometime . . .' We gained on him, being younger and lighter, and faster at sprinting up stairs. As we reached the open air his voice came up at us from the depths beneath, crying, 'Damn it, I only want to he . . . elp!'

The street was dark. It was a cold night. And as we stood hesitating on the pavement, the siren began its sickening wailing, warning of danger.

5

Out of the dark sky a noise was coming, a droning
sound. The streets were empty, there was no light.
Leaves blown across the pavement brushed our
ankles, and moved on, fleeing along the wind.

'Charing Cross Underground. Let's go there,' I
said, urgently. Grasping our blankets we stumbled
across the forecourt of Charing Cross Station, and
down the side street. Suddenly our path was bril-
liantly lit, bathed in icy white light. I saw her face,
a frozen mask, with pools of black fear for eyes,
framed in her dark hair, crossed by long wind-
blown strands. I reached out to her, and at arm's
length, brushed the loose hair back from her face.

Looking up we saw great globes of white flame floating in the sky, descending. Then a burst of loud gunfire from nearby, and darkness again, sudden and solid, like falling into a black pit.

'What's happening?' she cried to me.

'Those are enemy flares, parachute flares, shot out by our gunners. They are trying to get light to bomb by. Come on, come quickly now!'

Far off we could hear dull thuds, followed a few seconds later by a slight shudder in the air around us, a light rattle of window panes and doors. We could not see to run; we stumbled. Then at last we were there, staggering through the doorway into the familiar warmth and stench of safety. It was full there, crowded with people even on the District Line platforms and approaches, which weren't really deep enough to be safe. Still they gave at least a safety to the mind, keeping us from seeing and hearing, putting around us, like safety, the roofs and walls from whose weight we would die if the place were hit.

I put down the rucksack. And then we saw them. Three young men, and a shelter warden, and a grey-haired woman, paper and pencils in their hands, moving along the rows of families, talking, writing.

'Look,' I said to Julie.

'Oh, God,' she said softly.

'What do you want to do?' I asked her. 'Do you want to risk it?'

'Let's get out of here!' she said.

'No, let's give them phoney names and addresses,' I said. I was unwilling to go.

She shook her head. 'Not this time. I know one of them. That woman knows me quite well. It's Canada for me if she sees us.'

'Come on then,' I said, thrusting a blanket into the rucksack, stooping to pick up the other one.

'Bill,' she said in a quavering sort of voice, 'you could stay . . . It's me she knows . . .'

'Don't talk tripe!' I retorted. 'Get moving.'

Then we were out in it again. We stood in the doorway arch of the station, and she put the rucksack on my shoulders.

'Where are we going?' she asked.

'Waterloo is the nearest place, I think.'

'But it's the other side of the river!'

'Hungerford Bridge,' I said briefly. 'Come on.'

'That's a railway bridge,' she said.

'It has a footbridge,' I said. 'Who was the old dame, by the way?'

'Her? Oh. A teacher. My piano-teacher when I stayed with my aunt.'

We moved out again into the night. We clambered up the steps at the side of the bridge where it crosses above the Tube station, and while we climbed the night was quiet; only distant thumps and distant flares disturbed it.

At the top of the flight of steps there are some tall archways, looking out towards the east, with the footpath running along inside them. At the back of my mind I had thought we might shelter there; but they didn't feel safe at all, being high up and open. By the swiftly-passing light of a flare we could see posters on the walls, telling us it wasn't safe there; telling us where the nearest shelters were. Even when the flare was quenched we could see the poster; it just didn't seem to be dark. Ahead of us the path reached out in the open, hanging on the side of the bridge outside the girders of the upper work. Inside the cage of girders ran the railway. The path was narrow except where it had small bays on top of the columns over which the bridge was laid.

Slowly we edged out along the path, over the tops of the Embankment trees, out over the water. We went crouched down, so that the parapet shielded us. The parapet cast a deep shadow over us as we went – really it wasn't dark. The edges of the girders were traced in faint reflected light, and when a train rumbled by, shaking the ground we stood on, all the windows blacked out, we could see the criss-cross shadows of the girders moving across it.

We had nearly reached the second bay on the bridge when there was a tremendous bang on our left somewhere. Seconds later the air hardened into a wall, struck us, and lifted us, threw us against the fencing on the girders, and held us there. Somehow in the same split second, reacting to pain in my ears, remembering something I knew, I thrust the fingers of my left hand between my own lips, and those of my right hand into Julie's mouth. Turning her head, she tried to drag my hand away. I held on to her, fingers hooked over her teeth, while the air pressed down on us, held us spread-eagled, and crushed the breath out of us. Then we were being showered with specks of grit, which scratched our faces, and forced their way into our closed eyes; then the blast wave passed by, and the air dropped us, let us go, so that we slithered to the ground. On hands and knees we dragged ourselves into the lee of the parapet where it curved away from the line of the railway, making a small balcony over the river. And there we stayed. I was terrified. Not quaking with fear, but tingling with it – it was a prickling sensation on the skin, like having a high temperature. And although it was a cold night, with frost in the air, I was sweating. Yet I remember working it out quite coolly in my head; it was dangerous to stay where we were, but on balance more dangerous to move on.

Julie wriggled herself up close to the foot of the wall, and lay quite still, face turned skywards. We didn't say anything at all for a long time. We could hear a lot of noise: explosions, gunfire, and nearer to us, shrapnel winding down from the sky, making a funny sound like a gurgle with a whistle in it. After a little she said, 'You hurt my mouth.'

'If you don't keep your mouth open, the blast bursts your ears, I think,' I said.

'Oh, yes,' she said. 'I remember something about keeping a cork between one's teeth. Thanks, then.' Then, a lot later, 'Bill, are you all right?'

'Fine. Just a bit shaken. How about you?'

'All right. Bill, why isn't it dark? I wish it were dark!'

Very cautiously, I got up, and put my head over the parapet. I remember hearing my own voice, saying very slowly and clearly, 'God . . . in heaven . . . look at that!'

She moved. She looked too. Below us the water of the river was a sheet of orange and gold. The eastern sky, as in a monstrous sunrise, was an expanse of limpid golden light, as though the sky itself was a wall of fire. Against it we could see the slender spires of Wren's churches, and the great dome of St Paul's. They were not quite mere silhouettes; the corners, the columns, the curve of the dome had been traced in lines of reflected light, as though they had been drawn with a pencil of flame. London was burning. It was all on fire. The immensity of it quenched my own fear in a wave of awe; it seemed like the end of the world.

Our danger was only, after all, a small thing, seen in that light. I got right up, stood up, and pulled her to her feet too. Leading her by the hand I went on over the bridge, walking steadily. At the other end of the bridge was a little hut, a fire-watcher's post. In front of it a man was sitting, on a pile of sandbags. Round his neck hung a pair of binoculars, and a field telephone dangled in his drooped hand. His head was thrown back, so that the light of the burning city drew a circle of gold round his face, on the under side of the rim of his helmet. As we passed him I saw that his eyes were open, and the fire glinted in them too. They were still shining, still moist; he was very newly dead.

When we climbed down from the bridge we were in a warren of unfamiliar streets. I don't very well remember how long we wandered around there, but in the end we were found by a warden, who took us to a rest-centre; a grim sort of school building. It was like a very overcrowded shelter inside, or so it seemed at first glance. Then I saw that everyone there was filthy, covered with dirt and plaster, clothes torn and thick with dirt. A woman sitting at a table by the door said to us, 'Bombed out?'

Looking sideways at Julie, I saw that she was covered in sooty grime from crawling around on the bridge, and I supposed I was in the same state myself. 'Over there,' the woman said, without waiting for an answer. We went over there, and sat down. After a while someone brought strong black tea in chipped enamel mugs, and bread and jam. There was nowhere to wash. The people around us looked vacant, stunned. Children cried, and could not be quieted. We slept, almost at once, since sleep seemed the only good place to go.

We walked for hours the next morning. We didn't want to cross Hungerford Bridge back into the part of London we knew. There were lots of poor little streets over there, all knocked to blazes. Clouds of thick dust hung over the crushed buildings, and made a haze in the air everywhere. And it was all horrifying. The houses weren't abandoned, and boarded up, there were people everywhere. They scrambled around on piles of rubble, or came in and out of battered houses, carrying things. There were piles of furniture on the pavements; women sat on doorsteps, dabbing swollen eyes with the hems of their aprons. Puzzled and frightened children clung to them. We saw two women come staggering out of their house through a great hole in the wall, one carrying a dusty aspidistra in a pot, the other carrying a mantelpiece clock. They were smiling.

A little further down that street a woman was scrubbing her doorstep. Every window in the house was blown in, and the door hung crazily, blasted nearly off its hinges. But she was busily scrubbing her whitestoned doorstep, As we passed she called to someone across the street, ' 'Ave you seen the flaming milkman?' People, like trees, planted in their ways, persist absurdly in the same routines when everything is changed. Just beyond her two neighbours were talking.

'You go and shelter last night, ducks?'

'No I did not. 'Itler ain't goin' ter get *me* outer bed!'

'Whatser use? If it's got your number on it, it'll getcher anywhere. Rather die comfy in my bed, meself.'

On we went. On the next corner a dark blue lorry was parked, pulled up onto the pavement where it was wider in front of a pub. Two men were busy putting up boards, making cubby holes. The lorry was connected to a standpipe in a water hydrant in the road, and steam was drifting out of a little ventilator in its roof. It had LEVER BROS. SUNLIGHT SOAP painted on the side. A woman came out of the van. She was wearing a blue overall, and cap. Seeing us standing staring at it, she called out, 'You can have a bath in five minutes, dearie!'

A bath! The very thought of it! We waited. She went off down the road, and knocked on doors there. Soon more people were waiting, and women came up with buckets, and were given hot water from a tap. When the cubicles were ready they gave us towels and soap, and we had showers to bathe under. It felt marvellous to be clean again. I put on my last clean shirt, but it was horrible putting back the other clothes, all gritty with dirt. Julie emerged with her hair damp and sleek, hanging down like rats' tails round her shoulders. And somehow the night had washed away. We felt ourselves again, and we went back to the North Bank, looking for Marco's, though by now it would be lunch rather than breakfast, and we went by Westminster Bridge.

Marco's face lit up when he saw us. 'Amici!' he said. 'Marco worries for you. You no come, I think you go caput! You hungry, no? I get you good food, good coffee . . .' on he went, babbling away as usual. Julie afforded him a smile.

Sitting opposite her, at one of Marco's little tables, I saw a bruise on her lip.

'I hurt you last night,' I said.

'But I can still hear you say so,' she said, smiling. 'Does it look awful?'

'No,' I said. 'Not too bad. Take more than that to make you look awful.'

'Thanks!' she said, laughing.

'Julie, would you mind very much if we went back home, when we've eaten?' I asked.

'Back to your aunt's house? No, I don't mind. Do you want to see what's happened there?'

'No!' I said sharply. 'No, not exactly. I just want

to see somewhere that I know. I think I'd feel better for it, somehow.'

'Oh, I know what you mean,' she said. 'All right, let's.'

I still felt a bit guilty about it, as though I was putting something off that would sooner or later have to be tackled.

'Cheer up, Bill,' she said. 'We'll buy you a new shirt if it would cheer you up.'

I pushed the guilty mood away.

But of course, my aunt's house wasn't there any more. They had cleaned up some of the mess, so that the street was in use again, but where our houses had been there was nothing but a hole in the ground. And even worse, somehow, all the houses around were smashed; the views out of all the windows of our house had been swept away. It made me feel sick to the pit of my stomach.

'Bill,' said Julie, tugging me by the hand, 'don't keep looking at it. Don't keep looking like that!'

I still just stood and looked.

'Come on, Bill, there must be something round here you know, something still here. Come on.'

'There's a park I used to go to,' I said at last.

We wandered away down the street, towards the park. When I was much younger my father used to take me there, to get me out from under my aunt's feet, as he put it. I used to ride on the swings, and he used to smoke his pipe. The swings were still there, everything was the same there, even the familiar mist of an autumn afternoon, with the paint on the roundabout glowing against the whitened air.

Inside the palings we put down the rucksack, and then she sat on the roundabout, and I pushed it faster and faster, and then jumped on. There weren't any other kids there, but then it was so cold that wasn't surprising, and I suppose a lot of them had gone, now that so many houses were wrecked.

On the roundabout we laughed again, both of us.

'Make it go faster, Bill!' she cried to me. Jumping off I put my shoulders to it, leaning hard, and spun it faster and faster. Then I jumped on again for my own ride. The world whirled past so fast that it was just a blur; green and blue, smeared out of the sky and the grass, and men red and black, made of houses and fence. I looked round dizzily at Julie; since she was moving with me she was the only thing in the world in focus, laughing, with her hair flying out sideways, still heavy with damp

from the shower. Green and blue, red and black
. . . A smudge of khaki, seen and then not seen,
as the roundabout turned. A soldier was walking
along the road, behind the palings. And my heart
jumped. We were turning a little more slowly now,
and even though he was blurred by speed, even
though the glimpse of him walking was snatched
away and then shown again, I knew him. I jumped
to the ground. And the twist I had given that
damned machine seized me by the head, and my
head spun, and I stumbled blindly.

'Oh, don't stop, Bill!' cried Julie, disappointed.

'Oh, Julie, Julie, get off!' I cried in agony. 'That's
my Dad, that was my Dad!' It was already nearly
too late. He hadn't seen us. He was walking swiftly
away, and as my vision steadied I could see that
it was a long way to the next gate in the fence,
and he was already nearly at the corner. I took a
running jump, and landed on top of the fence,
balanced precariously on the top, between the
spikes.

'I'm going after my Dad!' I called to her, still
sitting on the slowly revolving boards.

'Goodbye, then, Bill,' she said, and gently the
roundabout turned her face away.

At the sound of emptiness in her voice I stopped.

I froze there, suspended. And it came to me very clearly that if I went after my father it was goodbye; it was just another way to Wales for me, and Canada for her. Or somewhere else for both of us, but wherever we went, not together. And there was Dad, hands in pockets, walking away, so far that I could no longer see anything of him but a figure in the crowd at the far end of the street, and if I looked away for a single minute I would lose him, and unless I jumped and ran now, now . . .

And there was Julie, in the park, all by herself, with a grubby rucksack, and two blankets, and nowhere to go, and nobody to go with . . .

I jumped down from the fence. I jumped back into the park.

I went and put my arms round a tree, and leant my forehead against it, pressing against the bark till it hurt. I was shaking, and bitterly ashamed of myself for that, and I didn't want anyone to see me, not *anyone*. So I stayed there a good while after the shaking stopped. She sat on the roundabout with her head bowed down, and it went very slowly and stopped, and she just sat there.

Then after a long while she came up and spoke to me. She said, 'I didn't mean it, Bill, really, I didn't mean to stop you, I didn't mean . . .' There were tear-marks smudged on her cheeks.

'You didn't stop me,' I said, as brightly and firmly as I could. 'Of course you didn't. I wanted to stay with you.' And after all, that was true. But my mind kept throwing up a picture of my father's back, receding down the street, and my thoughts bounced back from it, wincing.

It began to rain, then. First small heavy drops, then a downpour. We ran for a little wooden shelter on the far side of the swings, and sat in it, watching the rain make sulphurous yellow puddles in the sandpit, and dimple the undulating sand. We sat at either end of the bench in the cold little shelter, each separately looking out, silent. We listened to the busy noise of falling rain. And I was plunged into misery, and fear.

I wanted the houses I knew to be back up again; I wanted grown-ups to be there, I wanted to be told what to do; I wanted to be worried about, I didn't want to have anyone else to care for, I didn't want anyone to need me at all; I wanted to be back in Wales being yattered at, and given hot buns for tea; I wanted to be safe; I wanted my own father, I wanted my father, my Dad.

I couldn't bear to be responsible for anyone.

But there I was, there we were. And I couldn't leave her. And we had nowhere to go. I couldn't think where it would lead to, our being like that. I had thought I had come back to London to wait for my Dad; and now it seemed I hadn't been waiting for him at all. So what were we doing, and how would it end? Would I have to look after her for ever; would I never go back home? And where in hell were we going to sleep tonight?

'Oh, Bill,' she said, in a husky, choked voice, 'Bill, please, please don't be so miserable.'

I didn't answer. Did she expect me to be pleased about it?

'Oh, go and find him, then, go away, but don't stay and be so miserable!' she cried.

'I *did* stay, didn't I?' I said sullenly.

'I don't want you to, if you can't do it properly. I don't want to make you do things if you don't want to . . .'

'Oh, shut-up, can't you?' I said. 'It hasn't anything to do with you, bighead! Can't I feel miserable, if I bloody well want to?'

'Well, if it isn't me, what is it about?' she said, hanging her head.

'It's all right for you, isn't it?' I said savagely.

'*You* haven't seen your own house turned into a hole in the ground!'

She didn't answer at all.

'I'm sorry, Ju,' I said, after a while. 'I expect it's because I'm worried. I don't know what we're going to do. We shall have to spend some of your cash on new clothes sooner or later, and we can't possibly afford to stop working, and that means we've got to go back to the middle of town, and I don't know where we're going to sleep, or anything. We'll finish up getting ourselves killed.'

'Look, Bill, don't worry. I know where we can go. We'll be all right. We might get killed anywhere, you know. I might have gone to the bottom of the sea on that boat.' I felt too oppressed to ask questions.

'Right ho. Let's go to the place you know,' I said. We trudged away in the rain.

It was nearly dark when we got there. It was still raining, and it was cold. It was one of those London squares with four rather grand terraces of houses around it and a garden with railings round it in the middle. They hadn't pinched the railings for gun-metal yet. One side of the square had been badly bombed; the houses were in various stages of ruin, and it was here that Julie took me. She stopped on the pavement outside a house of which the front wall was still standing. The front door was still there too, but the windows were gaping holes, and through the upper ones we could see the sky. Broken glass and plaster littered the steps up to the door, and where there would have been steps down to the pavement there was just rubble, half covering the closed shutters of the basement windows, and burying the steps.

'Here?' I said incredulously.

'Come and see,' she answered. She walked up the steps, and produced a key from her purse. She gave it to me. It turned in the lock, but the door was a little stiff, and took a shove to open. I put my shoulder to it, and we stepped through. We stepped through into the open air.

The back of the house had collapsed; there were no floors and ceilings over our heads, and beyond the half-fallen walls of the hallway the debris rose in a crazy, rickety heap, leaning on broken timbers and slanting beams. The dividing walls between this house and the houses on either side still stood, bearing several different wallpapers and a number of fireplaces facing into the drop. And on our left the stairs still climbed from level to level of vacant space. Some of the banister-rails were broken. A chill wind blew through it all.

'Over here,' said Julie. She scrambled over the mass of broken banisters and glass which littered the hallway, and opened a door under the stairs. Steps led down. It was pitch black. 'I haven't been down here, but I think it might do,' she said.

'How the hell are we going to see?' I said, blinking.

'Wait a bit,' she said. She fumbled around in the dark. After a minute she found a cupboard, and opened the door. She put something into my hand, and then struck a match. It was a candle she had given me. The cupboard was a fuse cupboard, and it had a bundle of candles and a box of matches in it. By candlelight we descended the steps.

They led down into the basement of the house. There were two rooms there, back and front. All the windows were shuttered, and only two were broken. We knew that the front shutters were jammed up against all that fallen rubble, but I opened one of the back shutters all right. It was dusk outside, but a little grey light came in, and showed me a kitchen with sink, and oven range, and table like the one in my aunt's house, only bigger. There was even a dusty dresser, only most of the china had fallen off it and broken on the floor. The other room was a sort of shabby sitting-room, with a sofa, and armchairs, and a fireplace, and a window-seat with cushions on it running along under the shuttered windows. A little passage ran between the two rooms and the stairs, with a lot of cupboards built along it.

'Julie, how did you know about this?' I asked.

'It's my aunt's house,' she said, 'or was. This bit was where the servants lived.'

'Why ever didn't you tell me about it before?'

'Well, we were all right in the shelters, before those teachers came, weren't we? And safer.'

'Look, when you told me you had come here to look for your mother, and there was nobody there, you didn't say it had been hit.'

'It hadn't, then. It was quite all right, though the one on the corner had gone. But we came right past here the other day, and I saw it was like this.'

She hadn't said a word when she saw it. Girls are different, I suppose.

'Bill, do you like it? It'll be all right, won't it?'

'It's marvellous!' I said.

'So you will cheer up now, won't you?' she said, shyly.

'You bet!' I said. 'Let's have a good look round.'

'You look; I'll sweep,' she said. She went and got a broom from the cupboard, and started to sweep up the broken glass and china.

'You can't see much by that candle,' I said. 'I'm going back to the shops we passed, to buy a lantern:

'Try if the electric light works, first,' she said. It didn't, but the cold tap at the sink did.

It was getting cold as well as dark when I got back, with a paraffin lamp, and a can of juice for it. I stood it on the table, and lit it, and it made a bright warm light. Julie had found some unbroken cups and plates, and had set them out on the table.

'I'd better go out again, and see if I can find some food,' I said. 'Everything will be shut soon.'

'There are a lot of tins in the larder,' said Julie, 'We could try those. Come and see.' The larder contained masses of food; to me, used only to my aunt's thrifty housekeeping, it looked like a shop. There were tins of dried eggs and dried milk, some raisins in a jar, several sorts of tinned fruit, a large square unlabelled tin of lump-sugar, and four packets of tea, and lots and lots more. We felt like pirates finding Spanish gold. Rather cold pirates, with noses blue with cold.

'We could do with a fire,' I said thoughtfully, 'but I suppose the chimneys are all knocked to hell:

'I don't know,' she said, 'there are all those fireplaces still hanging on the side wall. We could try.'

I went up into the hallway, and brought down a handful of banisters, and sprinkled them with paraffin. We made a fire in the front room grate, and it drew beautifully, and the warmth and light it made were as welcome as summer. There was even a scuttle of dusty coal still standing beside the grate, with which we kept it going while we boiled a kettle on it. Then we pulled the armchairs up close to the warmth, and ate chunks of corned beef from a rusty tin, and drank cocoa made with hot water and dried milk, and lump-sugar, thick and comforting, and we drowsed there in blissful comfort.

When the fire began to die down, I got up and covered her with her blanket, and then curled up tightly in my chair under my own.

6

There was nothing to wake us the next morning; no light save a crack or two filtered round the shutters, and there were none of the disturbances as other sleepers woke and left. Julie woke me at last, pulling my blanket off me and letting the cold air sting me to life.

'Help me make a fire, Bill, and I'll get you something to eat!

I rose and stretched. She lit the lamp and we looked around. It all looked dirty and cold.

'I'll get some more wood,' I said.

In a little while we had a new fire going in the grate, and the kettle warming on it. I pulled a stool up to the windows, pushed down the top pane of the sash, and pulled away a broken slat in the shutter. The first one I tried let in a shower of pinkish dust, and I hastily jammed it back again; but higher up I managed to make a couple of slits which let in daylight. Then I went to the back room, opened the free shutter there, and opened the door between the two rooms.

The more light we had, the worse it all looked. It was incredibly filthy, with heavy deposits of white dust everywhere. The back room, where there was a usable window, looked pretty uninhabitable in every other way. I opened the door of the stove that warmed the oven, and the grate was choked with fallen brick and plaster. Not much hope of getting that going. And an icy draught blew under the broken back door. There was a huge damp patch on the ceiling, with the cracked plaster coming away, and dark wet marks on the floor beneath showed that the rain was coming through there heavily.

'This doesn't look much use,' I said to Julie.

'No,' she said. 'I'm going to move all the things that are any use out of here into the other room, as soon as we've had some grub. Help me find something we can eat.'

We found a tin of dried eggs, and some biscuits in a tin. There was a green mould on the biscuits, but it brushed off, more or less. The dried eggs were pretty nasty, but then they always are. We made more cocoa without milk. The kettle got so hot on the fire that we had to lift it off with fire-tongs, and it scorched the cloth we put over the handle to lift it and pour it out, but the water inside wasn't really quite hot enough, and so lumps floated on the cocoa.

'How far from here is Marco's?' I said, looking miserably at my plate. Still, however awful food tastes, it makes one feel stronger when it is safely tucked away.

'Look, Julie,' I said, pushing my plate away. 'It's two days since we did any work. We've got to keep earning money. I'm going back to the market. You coming too?'

'There's a lot to do here,' she said. 'Why have we got to keep on earning? Haven't we got any left?'

'Yes, we've got lots left. But even lots won't last for ever. We ought to keep it for special things, and try to earn every day what we spend on food. Then it won't get less so fast. After all, when it's gone . . .' I left the thought unspoken.

'All right, you go and earn some. You'd better leave me the rucksack money, because I'm going to need a primus stove. When shall I expect you back?'

I was disconcerted at being pushed off like this: I had wanted her to come too.

'Will you be all right here by yourself?' I asked, hopefully.

'Of course I will. I'll be too busy to worry. See you later.'

So off I went. As I went out through the shattered hallway, I saw the smoke from our fire, coming out of the first floor fireplace on the side wall, and drifting upwards. I wondered if it showed from the square enough to give us away. I crossed the square and looked back. But the smoke was so spread out by the time it rose above the façade of the house, that I thought one would only see it if one knew it was there, especially in the soft hazy weather of autumn. All the houses on our side of the square were gutted, and abandoned. We didn't have any neighbours. I was glad of that; I thought we had better try not to be seen.

It was a horrible day. A cutting north wind was blowing, and the stall keepers stamped their feet, and whistled into their upturned collars to keep warm. Money was short too, because nobody was shopping who didn't have to. I had a bit of trouble finding work, but Big Ben and Little Bert took me on for a couple of hours, mainly out of kindness, I think,

'How's the girlfriend?' asked Little Bert.

'Who? Oh, she's all right, thank you.'

'Bit of all right. Wouldn't mind myself, if I weren't too old for her,' said Little Bert, winking at me.

When my couple of hours with them were up, I went off looking for something else. The stalls were no good; they weren't taking enough money to be ready to payout any. But in a side street I found a frail old boy trying to put bits of furniture from a bombed-out house onto a handcart, standing in the gutter.

'A bob to do it for you, Guv,' I said. He looked at me thoughtfully, and sniffed. Then he painfully reached into his pocket, and brought out a handful of change, and turned it over, and muttered to himself, counting it. At last he said, 'Done.' By that time I felt a real swine for taking anything, and so when he got his things loaded up, I trundled the handcart round into the next street for him, and helped him unload it into a neighbour's garden shed.

By this time I was famished, as well as cold, and I bought myself a twopenny-worth of chips from the fish and chip shop, just chips, to save money. After that I found a cold-looking newspaper vendor at the entrance to an Underground station, and I offered to mind his stall while he went off to lunch. It was a pretty late sort of lunch, but he said he'd be glad of it.

Newspapers were selling all right; the war was good for that sort of trade. There was an air-raid warning while I stood there, but people didn't take much notice of it. And when he came back it was nearly four o'clock, and I thought I'd call it a day.

I was dead tired when I scrambled down the stairs to our den, and opened the door to the front room. And after all this time I can still see in my mind's eye what I saw then when I opened the door, and remember the astonished pleasure it gave me. A fire was burning brightly in the grate, and the paraffin lamp hung from a hook in the ceiling. Everything was clean and neat. The table from the other room had been pulled through, and put in one corner, and spread with a green-and-white cloth. There were plates, and knives, and forks set out there, and a loaf of bread. Beside the fire, on the tiles inside the fender, stood a little primus stove, with a pan simmering on it. The warmth of the room reached out and embraced me, laced with a slight smell of methylated spirit from the stove.

Julie looked up from a book, and smiled as I came in. 'Hullo, Bill,' she said. 'I'll just put some more coal on the fire, and then I'll serve up your tea.' I don't think in my whole life till then I remember being made to feel welcome, coming home.

The coal scuttle was full, and she piled a generous shovelful onto the flames. Then she picked up that pan, and brought it to the table, and took off the lid. A delicious meaty smell filled the room. She poured out thick ladlefuls of stew, and set the plate before me.

Then she began to serve herself.

'Julie, where did you get it all from?' I asked.

'All what?' she said, defensively.

'The meat. Meat is rationed. And the coal.'

'The coal is all right. It's from the cellar. There's a door that goes under the front steps, and through into a cellar under the pavements. It was a bit blocked up, but not too much for me to clear, and there's quite a bit of coal there!

'And what about the meat?'

She flushed. She picked up the pan, and turned

away from me, taking it back to stand in the warm. 'I found a ration book in one of the drawers there. They were all kept there, but one had slipped over the top of the drawer and fallen into the cupboard below. It must have got left when the others were taken. It's the cook's one. It's registered with a shop near here.'

'Well, but . . .' I protested.

'Well, we have to eat, don't we?' she said, tossing her hair back. 'And it isn't stealing. I paid for it!'

'It's someone else's ration.'

'But we aren't eating ours. Someone has got our books.'

'Oh, I suppose so,' I said, eating it readily enough. I didn't want to tell her what was really worrying me about it, which was that someone might check up. Perhaps the cook had got a new ration book, and someone might notice that she seemed to be drawing two rations. And if someone checked up . . . I hadn't a clue what would happen to us if we got found out. I supposed we must have broken a lot of regulations. I pushed the unwelcome thought away. But after all, it was for this, for her, that I had turned my back on Dad; and to lose it for a ration book . . .

When we had eaten we had to stand shivering

in the kitchen to wash up, with a kettleful of hot water. And then we went back to our warm armchairs. There was a card-table, with cards in a little drawer over under the window, and we pulled it up by the fire, and raced each other at clock patience. Then we found a jigsaw, and did that. Cook seemed to have had a passion for them, for there were about a dozen of them in her cupboard. I remember the picture we were making was of Trafalgar Square. Pigeons flew through it everywhere, and all the pieces were covered in feathers, and were hard to get in the right places. That was a good evening. It was wonderful just to be warm; just to have a real chair to sit in, and to be somewhere quiet, somewhere private, by ourselves.

Really, it amazes me to remember how comfortable we made ourselves there. I can see it as a pool of warmth and safety, I suppose because the paraffin lamp made such a glowing, friendly sort of light. It glinted on the china when we ate, and made our faces look smooth and soft. For a little while the burden of worry lifted from my mind, and rolled away, and I realized just how oppressed and anxious I had been. We had now no need to fear the onset of winter; we had no need to stay out in all weathers. And I was learning a good deal about the markets; I had a plan to mend the axle of a broken cart I had seen lying in a derelict place, and set up in business on my own. Like all the other streetmongers I could buy from Covent Garden market in the morning, and sell at a profit in the street. Then I would really be paying our way, and we could cease to fear the ending of her money, and the disaster that would bring.

I was planning it in my mind as I sat and warmed my toes by the fire.

And it worked out fairly well. There were drawbacks to the den, of course. There was a risk that someone living on the other side of the square might see us, coming and going, or spot our smoke, and might report us in some way to the faceless 'Them' of whom we were afraid. If I had known about street warden patrols I would have worried about them too. And food wasn't easy. We had to have lunch in a café, to save coupons, but there wasn't anywhere near enough to buy breakfast. Nearly everything was rationed, and one book wasn't enough for us. We ate a lot of bread, but we had pitifully little butter and marge to put on it. I remember breakfasts of one rasher of bacon, sizzled in a pan and shared between us, and five slices of bread apiece, wiped round the pan in chunks until the last smear of bacon fat had been eaten.

Another drawback was the raids. We could hear them much better on the surface. Instead of a distant thump or two, we could hear the crashing rumble of houses falling after the bangs. There was a warden's post just beyond the other side of the square, round the corner from the houses opposite, and we could hear motor bikes roar by, carrying messages, and hear the alarm bells of fire-engines and ambulances, hear people running and shouting outside.

But after the days we had just lived through, all drawbacks, all brief stabs of fear, were outweighed by a row of chestnuts roasting on the bars of our fire, and the feeling of wealth that having things that wouldn't go in a rucksack gave us. It was absurd, really, when the house above us was in such complete ruin, that all the things for cleaning and house-keeping in it were still safely stored away downstairs, but we found everything we needed. Julie washed our filthy clothes, and ironed them, and hung them on a clothes-horse round the fire to dry. We couldn't bathe there, but we found the Sunlight Soap van quite near us one morning, when the raids had been very near, and we got another bath from them.

I don't suppose it lasted much more than a week; at this distance of time I can only remember three evenings there. There was the jigsaw evening, and an evening when Julie had gone to Boot's Circulating Library, with Cook's ticket, and brought home books for us. She had chosen *The Master of Ballantrae* for me, because she knew I had brought *Kidnapped* away from home. Now I come to think of it, it must have taken me longer than one evening to read *The Master of Ballantrae*; but the bit I remember reading, with tingles of fear running down my spine, is the scene where they dig up his body in the moonlight, expecting him, hoping against hope for him to be still alive, and the Indian servant tried in vain to rouse him. I got to that bit late at night, when Julie was already asleep, and the fire had died right down to a mere smoulder, and the description of the pallor of death on the moonlit face gave me the creeps so badly that I found the sound of a raid outside almost a relief, since it took me out of the book and gave me something else to think about.

The third evening I remember, I started myself,

by bringing home a copy of the evening paper so that we could do the crossword after supper. I read the headline, but it didn't mean anything special to me. It said CITY OF BENARES SUNK – ALL FEARED LOST. But when Julie saw it she went as pale as paper, and just stood staring at it.

'Whatever's the matter, Ju?' I asked.

'That ship,' she said. 'It's the one I should have been on. It's sunk.'

I looked over her shoulder at the paper. The *City of Benares* had been carrying English evacuee children to Canada.

'Well, thank God you aren't on it,' I said. 'Thank God you ran away!'

'Don't you see?' she said wildly, looking at me with eyes brimming with tears. 'They think I am on it. Oh, my poor mother, she thinks . . .' The tears ran freely down her cheeks. 'Bill,' she said, 'I'll have to tell her, I'll have to go home now, I can't let them think . . .' She stopped. She saw the look on my face, and turned away. With her back to me, she said, 'Don't you think I should, Bill?'

I didn't answer. 'Bill, I must, musn't I?' she said, pleading.

'You have to make up your own mind about that,' I said, icily.

'No,' she said, turning to me, flushed, tear-stained, eyes unnaturally bright. 'No, you help me.'

'If you want to go, you damn well go!' I said. 'But don't expect me to say it's all right by me!'

She walked up and down the room, screwing handfuls of her skirt in her hands. Cruel and cold, I picked up my book, and pretended to read. In a little while she stopped opposite my chair, and said, 'Perhaps I could telephone, and just say I'm all right, and not say where I am at all . . .' Then her voice dropped, and she said, 'I suppose they'd start to look for me. They'd get the police in. They'd trace the call. They'd find us anyway . . .' I didn't look up from my book.

She began to pace the room again. Frozen behind my book, I was suffering hell. It was terrible to see her unhappy, to see her cry. Time and again I nearly said, all right, you go, tell them, I'll be all right . . . But I would not be all right. I wasn't unselfish enough to let her go. I stayed frozen behind my book. Later I remembered this, remembered that I could have let her go. I thought I had been punished for my selfishness.

She took most of the evening walking and crying. At last, very late, she came up to me, and pushed my book aside from my face.

'I shouldn't have let you do it,' she said, quietly. 'When you let your father go because of me, I didn't understand. I didn't realize how much it must have cost you. But since I let you do it for me, I have to do it for you.'

And I was so glad she would stay, so relieved, that I didn't really listen to exactly what she said, only to what it meant to me. And our supper was burnt and cold, and so nasty that we could only eat it at all by laughing over it.

The next day was the day we found Dickie. And in spite of all the bother he caused, it was just as well really, because it gave her something to think about, and me too, when I saw the expression in her eyes. There was always a certain expression in her eyes after that evening. It made me angry in a way; I was sure I hadn't carried on like that about my Dad.

We saw Dickie first when we left early one morning to go and look at the broken cart. I thought I might be able to make a new axle out of a piece of the banister-rail from upstairs, and we went together to have a look at it. There had been a raid the night before, behind the square, in a warren of poorer streets. And as we left, we saw a child, curled up on the pavement, sleeping against the railings of the square garden. We took no notice at all.

The cart had a broken handle as well as a broken axle; we found that as soon as we tried to move it. But the thickness of the banister was about right for the axle. It was a real old-fashioned job, just like a farm-cart, with the wheels fixed on with wooden wedges; and I thought I could manage to fix it, even though I wasn't exactly a handyman. Julie was keen to paint it, and put bunting on it, and make it look gay. She said people were so grateful for a bit of something cheerful to look at that they would come to us in hordes if we brightened it up a bit.

'Look, Bill,' she said, brushing at the sides. 'It had blue and yellow triangles on it once. We could touch them up again.'

'We have to get it mended first,' I said, protesting.

And when we got back after having lunch at a British War Restaurant, the kid was still there. He wasn't asleep any more, he was tottering about on the pavement, crying, and he looked as if he'd been doing that for a long time. As we passed him, an old lady came by, and she stopped.

'What's the matter, dearie?' she said to him.

'I want my Mum!' he said.

'Shall we go and look for her?' said the old lady.

'No,' he said, sobbing. 'She said wait here!'

'Well, then, that's what you must do, my dear,' she was saying, 'I expect she'll come back for you soon.' We closed our door behind us.

'Well, that kid's mother jolly well oughtn't to leave him waiting for her all that time!' said Julie indignantly. 'He's been there simply ages.'

And when I came out again, to go and buy tools and glue for the cart, he was still there, just leaning against the rails. It was beginning to rain. I bought the tools, and I went home, and I passed him yet again outside.

'That kid's still there,' I told Julie.

'Someone ought to take him somewhere,' she said. 'His mother obviously isn't coming back. She must have abandoned him.'

'Anything might have happened to her,' I said.

'He ought to be taken to the Child Welfare, or somewhere like that,' she said.

'Well, we can't do it,' I pointed out. 'A child welfare department is the last place on earth we want to be seen at. What if they asked about us?'

'Couldn't we tell fibs?'

'Surely someone else will take him soon.'

'There aren't very many people coming by here,

this side of the square, Bill, now that all the houses in the row are bombed.'

We sat down by our fire, and I began to shave the end of my treasured piece of banister, to fit the wheel-socket on the cart. But we could hear the rain dripping through the ceiling next door, and pattering on the shutters, and after a bit we couldn't bear it. So I got up, and went out, and crossed the road, and picked up the kid in my arms, and carried him in.

He was soaked to the skin, and shivering. Julie took all his clothes off, and wrapped him up in her blanket, while she dried them on the clothes-horse.

'What's your name?' she said to him softly, very gently, 'What's your name?'

'Dee . . . kee . . .' he said. So we called him Dickie. But 'Dee . . . kee . . .' was what he said to anything, any time – to us. He never talked to us as we had heard him talk to the woman on the pavement. There seemed to be something wrong with him.

At first, I think, he was just scared. He jumped every time we moved, or even put a cup down. When night fell he stirred in his sleep every time a bomb fell, and I stirred too, uneasily aware of the extra person in the room, and the extra problem he gave us. Julie had made a bed for him by pushing a chair up beside the window seat, to stop him rolling off, and laying him there on the dusty cushions, covered with my jacket and her mac.

In the morning we talked about him again. 'We've got to think of a good way of handing him over to someone,' I said.

'All right,' she said, challenging me. 'How shall we do it?'

'Well, we could take him somewhere, and leave him for someone to find.'

'Oh, Bill, really! He was left for more than a day for people to find, when we found him. Fat lot of good that did!'

'Oh, well, I suppose that would be a bit callous. Then we must take him ourselves. We take him to the Welfare, or a warden's post, or the police station, and just say we found him on our way to the shops. And we give them phoney names and addresses if they ask. Just the number of any bombed house will do. That would cover our tracks nicely.'

'And what happens to him then?'

She startled me. The only snag I foresaw in my suggestion was the chance that something would happen to *us*. 'Well, *I* don't know,' I said. 'I'm not an expert, am I? They'll see to him. It won't be any business of ours, anyway.'

She just looked at me, coldly. I felt myself flinching under her coldness.

'Hell, Ju,' I said, 'I'm sorry for the poor little blighter too, but he'll be all right. They'll put him in an orphanage, or somewhere.'

'Yes,' she said, icily. 'I dare say they will.'

'Well . . .' I muttered, helplessly.

'Well, how would you like being stuck in an orphanage?'

'I don't *know*!' I said. 'I suppose they're all right.'

'You brute,' she said.

She made me remember something. Something hidden a long way down. A time when we first moved in with my aunt, and I used to creep out of bed at night, and sit at the top of the stairs to watch the pattern of light made on the frosted glass on the landing window when cars passed by outside. I heard voices downstairs, my father and my aunt talking with voices raised.

'You are too hard on him, Meg . . . He's got to have somewhere to play. He didn't make much mess, really.'

'You should try clearing it up!' said my aunt.

'I do what I can,' said my father, 'but I'm not here all day.'

'Look here, John,' said my aunt, much more softly, in a weary sort of voice. I had to lean my head down, towards the hall, pressing my face against the banisters, to hear her still.

'If I hadn't taken you both in, he'd be in a Home. He would be made to toe the line all right, in there. I may not be all you'd want, but I'm better than a Home. You just remember that when you're finding fault with me.'

My father said, 'God knows. I'm grateful to you, Meg . . .' Obscurely frightened, I had crept back to bed,

'They can't *all* be so awful!' I cried.

'I've got a friend at school who was in one till the better-off side of her family heard about it. They came driving up, late at night, and her cousin's mother was *crying*, she was so sorry to have let it happen, and they took her away right then, and looked after her.'

I felt very tired. A great weight of worry, worse than ever, seemed to have been laid on my shoulders.

'I'm sorry for him, Ju,' I said. 'Honestly I am. But we can't look after him here. We just can't.

We haven't the money for another person. We haven't the coupons. We haven't the strength. We can only just keep going ourselves. And it isn't our fault what's happened to him. 'It's just his bad luck.'

She didn't answer that at all. She turned away, and wiped his nose for him.

After a bit I said, 'So what do you suggest, anyway?'

'I think we should look after him here, until he trusts us, and remembers how to talk. Then we can find out where his mother is.'

'But it might take ages. He might never remember. And if he does, don't you see that she's probably no good to him now?'

'What do you mean?'

'She's probably dead!'

'We could wait and see. His whole family can't be dead.'

'I'm sorry, but we can't. We can't manage. I'd keep him out of an orphanage, just like you would, if we could, but we can't, and that's all there is to it.'

'No it's not,' she said, facing me squarely. 'Because we *can* keep him out. We could telephone my aunt, and she would find my mother, and they

128

would help him. It's all very well, managing by ourselves; but I don't call it managing if it makes us do hateful things that we wouldn't have to do otherwise! '

The pit of my stomach lurched, and tightened. The ground seemed to drop away from under my feet. I just about managed to steady my voice, or thought I had, but it came out very odd sounding. 'Is that what you want to do?'

She said, 'Look, Bill, I know how much you want us to stay here. I'm ready to stay with you. But I won't have anyone else, like Dickie, suffer for it. We have to manage as well by ourselves as we would with the grown-ups, otherwise we ought to stop.'

I went and sat down in my armchair, and put my head in my hands. That child had been listening to every word we said, though I don't suppose he understood. He was an odd-looking little beggar, about three feet high, with dark red hair, a bit curly, and brown eyes. They looked sad, and rather vacant, like cow's eyes.

In the end I said, 'Well, I think we could support Dickie too if we make the barrow scheme work. If it's still odd-jobbing, and with you always at home to look after him, we won't be able to manage. We'll try. If the barrow doesn't work, we'll give in.'

She said, to comfort me, 'We wouldn't have to give in at once. We could spend the rest of my money first.'

I didn't reckon we could. If she was going back to her parents, I reckoned we ought to have as much as possible of their fifty quid to return to them, otherwise I might find myself in really nasty trouble.

The barrow was our only hope. It was the best hope for Dickie too, come to that, because I didn't feel as sure as Julie seemed to do that her mother and aunt would jump to the rescue of a totally strange waif and stray. But I felt a long stab of regret about it all. I hadn't imagined myself being a green-grocer. I had wanted to be an engineer.

7

It took me the whole of the next day to finish tapering the ends of the wooden axle. The banister-post I was working on was oak; that made it hard to work on, but I thought it would also make it strong enough for the job. Dickie liked the chips and shavings that came off; he sat around on the floor and played with them. At lunchtime I went out and bought fish and chips for us; I didn't say anything, but with a sinking heart I had foreseen another snag to Dickie; we wouldn't be able to take him into cafés without attracting attention, and one ration book wasn't going to feed three of us with homecooked food. Perhaps at British

Restaurants, where families ate together very often, we would be able to take Dickie with us without being noticed.

For the moment the axle was problem enough. I slung it on my shoulder, and trotted off with it, and then when I got it to my cart, I found I couldn't pull away the broken one. I struggled with it for a while, but I knew I would have to get help. That was a bit tricky; I didn't know who the cart belonged to. Pinching it was one thing, getting somebody to help me pinch it was quite another.

I thought about it for half-an-hour, and then I went to see Big Bert and Little Bert. Their stall was in the usual place. I told them about the cart, and asked them to help. They said they would come along at lunchtime.

'Whose is it, then?' said Big Bert, as soon as he saw it. My heart sank.

'Mick's. It's Mick's old one,' said Little Bert. ''E's in the army; 'e don't want it now. 'E can always ask for it back when 'e comes 'ome, can't 'e?'

'Rightcheware,' said Big Bert. 'Give us a 'and, then.'

They knocked the wheelcaps off with a blow from my new axle, and then the old one slid out as easy as pie.

'Easy, when yer knows,' said Big Bert, smugly. 'Just run back and fetch us a 'ammer, Bert, willyer?'

Together Big Bert and I turned the cart over, on its back. Then we pushed the new axle through, and rolled the wheels up, and lifted them on to the projecting ends of the axle. We tried them, and they wouldn't turn. Big Bert lifted one off again, and looked at it. The ball-bearings in a runnel on the inner edge of the wheel, where it turned against the axle, were stuck fast in a thick black sludge of old dirt. They weren't moving. He prised them out with his penknife, and scraped out the dirt.

'I've got some oil, Bert,' I said, producing a small tin of bicycle oil from my pocket.

'Watcher going ter do wif that?' he asked, grinning. 'Oil yer eyeballs?' But Little Bert had thought to bring a tin of grease as well as the hammer. Once more we lifted the wheels into place. I held the wheelcap over the axle end, and Little Bert held wedges in place, and Big Bert bashed them with the hammer until they were forced in between the wheelcap and the axle, and the wheel was held onto the end of the axle.

'You done a good job on that axle,' said Little Bert, and I felt proud.

We fixed the other wheel on in the same way.

'How about the broken 'andle?' asked Little Bert.

'I've got this bit of wood, and a ball of string,' I said. 'I'm going to lash it onto the broken bit, like a splint.'

'Good idea. That'll do it,' said Big Bert. 'Well, now you got a cart, what you going to do with it?'

'Sell fruit and veg, I hope,' I said. I couldn't help looking at them anxiously, to see if they thought it would work

'Why not?' said Little Bert.

' 'E'd better go and see Old Riley,' said Big Bert. 'Look 'ere, Bill, you go and see Old Riley. They'll tell you where he is if you ask at the Garden. Tell 'im you're a mate of ours; 'e'll let you have a bit of stuff.'

'Thanks,' I said.

'Oh, and just a word with yer,' said Little Bert. 'Mate of mine got into a spot of bother on 'is first stand. Got beaten up something 'orrible. Month in 'ospital. Know what 'e done?'

'No,' I said.

' 'E put 'is barrer right beside another geyser's, and asked for a penny less for everythink. Doesn't do. Keep your eyes skinned for other fellers' prices.'

'Thanks,' I said.

'Talk lovely to the coppers, and you'll be all right there too,' said Big Bert. 'Tata. See yer.'

So then I bound up the broken handle, and trundled the cart off home. It squeaked at first, and moved jerkily, but by the time I got it home it was moving smoothly and sweetly. It would have stuck out like a sore thumb, parked on the pavement outside the house, so I took it round the back. There was a sort of lane that led between the walls of the gardens, not that they were gardens, really, only yards, and the cart fitted down there, though only just. It kept bumping the walls as I wheeled it. I pulled it up onto the rubble where Julie's aunt's garden had once been, and proudly went to fetch Julie to look at it.

'I've got something to show you, too, Bill,' she said. She had bought two tins of paint. *Durable Gloss* in blue, and in yellow. 'And I found this too,' she said. 'This' was a table-cover, a dark rust colour, and thick, like a rug with a deep pile. People used to keep them over the table in the parlour; my aunt had one.

'Well, so what?' I said, mystified.

'I thought it would do to cover the barrow with, to set off the fruit,' she said. 'The real costermongers have that sort of green stuff, that looks like grass, but I couldn't think how to get some of that.'

'This will do fine,' I told her.

Most of the rest of the day we spent painting. We could just see the old pattern, but it wasn't as easy as it looked to paint it the same again; it was jolly hard to get the edges straight, and then we hadn't the sense to see that you can't have both colours wet at the same time, so soon we had a lot of green smears, wherever the two colours met. After a bit we just made it marbled, like the endpapers of an old book, and it looked quite bright and jolly like that.

It would have been fun painting, if it hadn't been for Dickie. He wanted to be with us, and he cried, and clung to Julie's skirts if she tried to leave him indoors, but he seemed very cold outside, and shivered a lot, and made a sort of grizzling noise, non-stop, till I could have sloshed him. We tried our best to cheer him up, but it *was* rather cold out there. We had pinched fingers, and red noses, and plumes of breath floating foggily around our faces. We tried to cheer him up by letting him have a go with the brush, but he just held it, drooping from his small red hand, and big blobs of clear yellow dripped off it, and made sun-shaped splashes on the rubble at his feet.

As the afternoon went on he stopped crying, and just sat, gloomily watching us, and he got paler and paler, till he looked really ill. At last Julie took him in while I did the last bit myself. There was a cloudy blue dusk thickening round me, and the siren howled overhead as I finished.

There was a pot of tea ready when I went in, and a loaf of bread, and a little jar of dripping from the butcher round the corner to eat it with. Julie had had time to warm up, and she looked glowing and fresh from the raw open air of the afternoon, but Dickie looked funny. He wasn't pale any more, he had two round very bright red splotches on his cheeks, like a painted doll, and his eyes were glittering and bright, I glanced from him to Julie, and as if she caught my anxiety she went to him and said, 'Tea-time, Dickie. Do you want some tea?'

He shook his head, but she picked him up, and carried him over to a chair.

'Dickie,' she said to him, 'Is this what your mother gives you for tea, when you're at home?' He didn't answer. 'Where do you live, Dickie? You can tell us. Bill and I are your friends.' He didn't answer. 'What's your other name, Dickie? Dickie what?' It was no good.

'Perhaps he doesn't understand the words we use,' I suggested. 'Perhaps he doesn't know what home means. Dickie, where do you sleep? Can you show us where your bed is?'

Slowly, laboriously, he clambered down from the chair, and staggered over to the window seat. He leaned down onto it and said, 'Dee . . . kee.' We gave up.

He wouldn't eat any tea, either, but just lay there.

'He isn't well,' said Julie. 'Perhaps he needs a doctor.'

'We can't call a doctor, here,' I said. 'We could take him to one, tomorrow.'

'We might have to,' she said. But all evening Dickie slept, though he moved restlessly.

It really was a bitterly cold night: we got frozen washing up the plates in that horrible kitchen. It had got worse, for a hole had appeared in the ceiling where the damp had been coming through, and cold air blew through it now. When we had finished we went and sat on the floor right in front of the fire, side by side, warming our backsides at some risk of scorching our clothes.

'Bill, is there anything you miss much?' she asked.

'From the way things used to be? I don't know really. Haven't thought. How about you?'

'Oh, this and that,' she said, off-hand.

'Like what?'

'Bacon for breakfast, and butter for tea.'

'Gosh, yes. But we wouldn't have those now, anyway, or not often, with everything rationed.'

'I had bright flowered wallpaper in my room, and the sun used always to shine on it in the morning. I miss that. Come to think of it, I think living in a room with daylight in the daytime is what I miss most.'

'I think I miss school quite a bit,' I said, after giving the question some thought. 'I used to think I didn't like it, but now it isn't there any more, I see that I did. It had nice easy rules.'

'Yes,' she said, 'and poetry lessons.'

'*Poetry?*' I said, in loud disbelief.

'Well, I didn't like the actual lessons. It embarrassed me a bit, to see silly old Miss Hinds, waltzing round the room saying "Claads of golden daffodils" with the book hugged on her chest.' I began to laugh. 'But I like the way bits of it come back to you later, and seem terribly true; you know, like

139

when you're lying in the bath. Now that's a thing I miss – a real bath you can lie in.'

'You mean, like "I am the Master of my Fate, I am the Captain of my Soul"?' I asked.

She looked dubious. 'Well, not quite like that,' she said, laughing herself.

'Anyway, some things are better,' I said. 'Like having company.'

'You haven't any brothers or sisters, Bill, have you?' she said.

'No.'

'I thought not.'

'Even if I had . . .' I began, but I thought better of it.

In the end we got pins and needles, sitting on our heels like that, and we had to get up and hop about a bit. It was then that we noticed that Dickie was shivering. His little form was shaking under the jackets so violently that we could see it from the other side of the room.

We went to him. He looked terribly ill now. His body, his legs, his hands were ice cold, so that they were a shock to the touch, but the nape of his neck and his forehead were burning hot. His shivering was steady, unremitting, and his face was damp with sweat. His hair was darkened, almost brown, and stuck to his scalp.

'My God, Ju,' I said, 'what shall we do with him?'

'Get him warm,' she said, tersely.

We lit the primus stove, and put a kettle on to boil. We pushed our chairs right back from the fire; we raked it, and piled on more coal. We laid cushions on the floor in the pool of warmth just in front of the grate, and carried him over from the window, and laid him there. When the kettle warmed we filled Cook's hot water bottle, and put it beside him. Julie pulled a pile of clean dusters out of a drawer, and we dipped them in warm water, and wrapped them round his hands and feet, and then dipped them to warm them up again. After a bit of this we stopped, and rubbed him dry. He just lay there, letting us do things. He looked at the ceiling, if he was looking at all.

'We need some grease, or something,' said Julie, looking round. We got the remains of the dripping from tea.

'Put just enough on your hands, so that they slip, and then rub him,' she said. We bent over him together, she rubbing his chest, and I rubbing his hands and feet. In the end we got him warm enough to seem human to the touch.

'Blankets,' said Julie. I brought hers and mine, and we put them over him where he lay. For a little while he lay there, following Julie with his eyes. Then slowly his lids drooped, and he fell asleep.

'Dickie?' she whispered, very softly. He did not stir. 'Thank heavens!' she said, 'he's asleep.'

'Is there any water left in that kettle, Ju?' I asked. 'I'll make you a cup of tea.' It was while we were drinking it that I said, 'That air-raid warning earlier on was a bit of a dud, wasn't it?' and with uncanny promptness there was a shattering bang, very near us, that made us both jump from our chairs. With a swift *woomph* noise the shutters pushed inwards against their bolts, and then slackened. An avalanche of rubble started to pour through the hole in the ceiling next door, clattering and rustling for what seemed endless minutes; then silence except for gunfire, further away.

'Don't say that sort of thing!' cried Julie. I was afraid our way out might have been blocked, but when I went to look there was only a pile of debris a couple of feet deep decorating the kitchen floor, and a yawning hole above it through which I could see the stars.

I went back to Julie. Distant thumps and bangs, the usual noises of a raid, reached us from outside, but after the near one we were more nervous about it than usual.

'Time we got some sleep,' I said.

Our blankets were wrapped around Dickie, still sleeping peacefully on the hearth. We had to bank the fire down with a thick layer of coal dust if it was to keep in all night; burning brightly it would burn out in a few hours. Banked down it gave much less warmth, and our chairs were further away from it than usual, with Dickie in the way. And he had our blankets. Gloomily we settled down, she under her mac, in one chair, me under my jacket in the other.

We couldn't sleep at all. It was too cold.

My feet were like blocks of ice. I tried curling them up underneath me somehow, but I couldn't. After a bit I got up, and made some cocoa with horrid dried milk. Julie, wide awake, and shivering, drank some too. Then we tried again. Dickie seemed so soundly asleep that we turned out the lamp, and lay shivering in the dark. Sounds of the raid jolted us every few minutes.

In a silent interval I could hear Julie a few feet away, her teeth rattling in her head.

'Ju?'

'Mmm?'

'You all right?'

'Oh, Bill, I'm so cold it *hurts*!

'I can't get to sleep either.'

'I've tried thinking about warm things, and it doesn't work at all; I wonder what people do in the Arctic?'

'That's it!' I said. 'Good idea. They get in each other's sleeping bags. Come on, let's push the chairs together.'

'We can't do that,' she said. Her voice was shaken by shivering.

'That's what they do. Honest, I read it somewhere.'

'Maybe,' she said.

'Come on, Ju,' I said. No reply. 'It'll be all right, I promise. I can't bear to see you so cold.' I lit the lamp again. She had got up, and was standing by the table, hugging herself from cold, looking very miserable. I pushed the chairs together, and they made a sort of bed, and I got the jacket and the mac. She didn't come, so I lay down there myself, and put the light out. After a bit, when the noises outside got louder again, she came too.

She was much colder than me; ice to touch. She

seemed to be trembling all over. I sat up, and put my jacket on, and then lay close to her, and buttoned it round her too. Then I pulled the mac over us both, and put my arms round her. She shifted, looked for somewhere to put her own arms, and round me was the only place. Then I shivered a bit myself, I suddenly wanted to crush her, to hold her so hard it hurt us both, but I knew it would frighten her, so I lay still. And slowly warmth grew under the mac, and thawed the cold of her hands and feet. Her hair spread out on the cushion near my face, and it smelled faintly of the coal-tar soap from the bath van. Soon it seemed to me that not only the aching coldness of my limbs, but the entire weight of my body, and every painful or harsh feeling I had ever known, had melted away in a cocoon of warmth, in which we floated into sleep.

Dickie woke us. As soon as we surfaced from sleep we could hear that all hell was let loose a little way off somewhere, but it was Dickie who had woken us. He was staggering around stumbling in the dark, crying. I sat up abruptly, and Julie, who was still buttoned into my jacket was jerked awake with me. The faintest possible fingers of grey light slanted through the shutters, but I leaned over, and lit the lamp, with Julie's sleepy head on my shoulder getting in the way. Then with some light to see by, we disentangled her.

Dickie was still tottering around; then his legs folded up and he fell to the floor. Almost at once he doubled up, and made a small choking noise. When Julie lifted him he was being sick. He hadn't eaten very much the day before, so his stomach was empty. Doubled-up and choking, he was bringing up only a clear ropey fluid like spittle.

'He needs a doctor,' said Julie, helplessly, holding him in her arms.

'We can get him to one when the day gets started,' I said, knowing that surgeries didn't begin till nine. 'But what can we do for him now? Surely there must be something we can do for him now.'

'Perhaps some milk would settle his tummy,' she said. I lit the stove for her to make some milk. We were using only dried milk, because fresh milk was rationed. We could hardly have asked the dairy to send a milkman round to us, anyway. Julie mixed and warmed the stuff, and sat Dickie on her knee, offering him the cup. A great bang and rumble, nearby again, shook the houses. For a moment our attention switched to the noise outside, and I said, 'I hope to God my cart's all right!'

Dickie grabbed the cup, and drank greedily,

stopping only to take breath, in fierce little gasps, and then drinking again. When he had taken it all, he leaned back against her, looking almost happy, but then a few seconds later he flung himself across the arm of the chair, and was sick again. Julie went for a cloth and a bucket.

'That beastly powder hasn't dissolved properly,' she said, kneeling to wipe it up. 'No wonder he couldn't take it. But I think it was the right idea. We have to get him some fresh milk.'

I said, 'I'll get some.' An angry outburst of gunfire rattled overhead. She was kneeling in front of the fire, holding Dickie in her arms, her face upturned to me over his shoulder.

'There hasn't been an all-clear,' she said.

'Where do you keep the book, Ju?' I remember my voice was strangely softened, my face felt smooth and calm and her face too looked shining and serene. It seemed to me we hadn't come apart properly when we rose from sleep, but in some way we moved together still. I was ready to do anything, like a god, and she knew that I would, and her trust shone clearly in her eyes.

'In the top drawer,' she said. 'Take care.'

Then I left her, and climbed out into the open.

* * *

I stood on the top step, in front of our absurd front door, and looked across the square. The square itself was hushed, full of that dim grainy light that precedes sunrise. Far away I could hear the unceasing guns; but nearer, behind the houses around me was another sound, the soft disturbance of silence, the rustlings and murmuring that suggest movement, people, things happening.

I looked up, and saw across the sky the loops and lines, the crazy scribblings of vapour trails, touched with the first morning light, shining silver like frost, a murderous tinsel festooned over the grey city. It entered my head that I ought to go and see that the cart was all right, that I had to get to Covent Garden early, and ask to see Old Riley, but I pushed the thought aside. Milk for Dickie first. I thought I knew where the milk depot was, for I had seen empty milk vans returning in the afternoon, the patient horses plodding along, with empty nosebags hanging from their bits. I turned my collar up against the cold, and set off.

I saw I wasn't going to get there as soon as I turned into the street where I thought it was. The end of the street was blocked by a great wall of smoke, the windows on either side down there were squares of solid fire, people were running

148

about shouting, fire engines were drawn up, fire hoses ran up and down along the street, dozens of them, great tangled snakes, tripping everyone as they ran. Overhead the trolley-bus wires ran towards the fire, and then dangled in a molten tangle from a sagging post. Down there by the smoke-wall firemen pointed hoses into the blaze, dark ropes of water, arching criss-cross over the street. I saw two men stagger a little under the backward thrust of the hose they were directing, and the water jet looped the loop in the air. I wasn't going to get past. I turned away, and then there was a shout, and I turned round just in time to see the front of the building collapse. It leant forwards, all in one piece, like the front of a doll's house being lifted away, and then it bent at the knees and came down in a roar. People ran in all directions away from it.

Well, there must be another way round to the depot. I tried the next street. That was shattered. One could hardly see where it had been; it was just a shallow valley in a sea of rubble, under a cloud of choking dust. Grey figures walked over it, looking for places to dig. Above us the planes still droned. I tried the next street, but by then I knew the depot must have been hit, and I would have to try somewhere else. Where else? I could look for a milkman on his rounds, but if the nearby depot had been hit, I would have to go some way to do that. Then I thought of Marco. If I was going some distance, I might as well go there, and be sure of getting some. Marco would help. I started to walk, but after a little while a bus lumbered along the road, and I hailed it and got on. It was nearly empty, and it had four windows broken, but it was going the right way.

'You got hit,' I said to the conductor.

'It's hell back there,' he said. 'But we're on time, know that, mate? We're even on the bloody schedule!' Then he leant out from the platform, and yelled like a maniac at the sky, 'We ain't even late, tell that to bloody 'Itler!' I sat and looked through a broken window. The streets were full of people. Bowler-hatted and black-umbrellaed, they were coming to work, stepping gingerly over fire hoses, and round craters, looking around at the damage as they went. Then it was my stop, and I got off.

Marco's was boarded-up and closed. The whole row of shops where Marco's had been was gutted. I panicked. The thought of the time I had wasted made me feel sick with rage. I vaguely wondered what had happened to Marco, and his moon-shaped smile, but I had precious little time to waste wondering about him. I thought despairingly that I would have to go back without the milk, and just wait for the doctor's surgery to open. But really I knew I couldn't do that. I had turned my back for ever on not being able to do things when I let my father pass by. Now I was on my own, and I had to do whatever had to be done. Julie said we had to manage as well as grown-ups, or else stop trying at all; she thought I could do it. It had to be done.

I made for the Underground. The trains were running, but they were maddeningly slow. At every station people getting off and people getting on tangled with sleepers, with camp breakfasts, or had to walk narrow gangways between bunks. It seemed ages to me before I got back.

Above ground again, I started to walk. I told myself that if I saw a bottle of milk on a doorstep, I would steal it, and solve the problem that way. I did not see one. A thick blanket of low cloud had followed the dawn across London, but behind it the planes droned on, and I could hear explosions, feel the jolt in the air. I think a blast wave knocked me down at one point; I don't exactly remember it, but I remember clambering up again, and walking on. I walked. I stopped people, and asked them where I could find milk. They didn't seem to know. The air seemed dense, smoky, foul. It was like fog, where I was walking; you couldn't see very far, and people lurched at me through the gloom, and gave crazy answers to my desperate questions. Perhaps being knocked down by a blast wave had made me a bit duffy for a while, for I don't remember it very clearly. I remember stopping people who were staggering along, filthy, with scratched faces, and hardly any clothes on. Blast tore people's clothes off, and they must all have been reeling with shock, and there was I, half demented, asking them where to find milk.

I walked on, towards the place all these people were coming away from. I was going along a street with lots of narrow low terrace houses, with doors straight onto the pavements. There was a lot of mess on the street, and no windows left anywhere. The houses had no roofs on. The street was still, deserted. And then I passed by the window of a room with someone in it. I stopped and looked in. The room was a kitchen, with a woman in it, sitting at the table. She was sitting in a rocking chair, rocking very gently. She was wearing one of those cross-over flowered aprons, and a headscarf round her head, with the knot tied on top. The table had things laid on it, and a fine dust was raining in the room. Plaster was filtering through the rafters from upstairs. But what my eyes fixed on was a glass jug, standing on the table, full of milk.

I went in. It was quite easy, her front door wasn't there any more. I went in, and said to her, 'Please, missus, could you let me have a little of your milk?'

She didn't answer. She looked at the window, with eyes full of dust. She was stone dead, with the milk unspilled in the jug in front of her. I looked at it. A thick scum of dust floated on it. I opened the drawer in the table and there were all her spoons and knives, laid out in rows, as she had left them. I took a spoon, and skimmed the milk with it, scooping away the dust and the cream. And while I did it, I talked to her, very gently.

'It's for Dickie,' I told her. 'He can't take the dried stuff, he's not well. You don't mind very much do you? It's for a sick child. I wouldn't take it for myself.' I picked up the jug, and held it under my jacket. I said to her, 'I'm sorry about it. I'm sorry about you. But you have a nice sort of face. Even all dusty. I don't think you would have minded, anyway.' A gust of wind came through the gaping window, and gently rocked her in her chair. Clutching the milk, I went.

I had quite a walk back. Dimly, I was aware of things happening round me, ambulances, fire-engines, bangs, hoses, but I walked in a dream, sheltering the jug of milk in my jacket, concentrating on not spilling it. Once a warden ran up to me, as I walked steadily through a cloud of smoke, and said, 'Are you all right, son?' in an urgent tone of voice.

'Perfectly,' I said.

'Where are you going?' he said.

'Home.' He left me. He had worse cases to bother with. On I went.

I suppose I noticed as soon as I entered the square that it looked different. But I went: on for several minutes, doggedly plodding towards it, before I really saw. Then I noticed, in the far distance, my cart, perched upon the rubble, and I was glad it was all right. And then I dazedly wondered how I could see it, when it was behind the row of houses; then I finally came to my senses, and saw what I saw.

It had all gone – the whole row of damaged houses had collapsed. There was no front door, no steps, no shutters visible above the rubble. There was only a great mound of broken brick, dust, and splintered timber. The whole of our hideout was deeply buried.

The glass jug shattered at my feet, and the milk splashed me, and ran in rivulets across the dirty paving stones. I looked at it in faint surprise; I had not remembered letting it fall. Overhead there suddenly sounded the steady, cheerful note of the all-clear.

8

I ran. I ran round the square towards the warden's post, ran and stumbled, my knees feeling like water, and my feet like lead. I was running straight towards all my enemies, the wardens, the welfare, the teachers, the police, anyone, anyone who could help.

Just round the corner was a little hut on the pavement heavily covered with sandbags. Over it rose a scaffolding, with the siren mounted on it. I burst into it, not bothering to knock. A man was sitting there, in a cramped little room lined with shelves. Ropes, lamps, boots, all sorts of things were neatly lined up on the shelves. A street map hung facing him, and he sat at a rickety table with a telephone on it, pads of paper, and a big book lying open. There were other men there too, tin-hatted and blue-canvas-suited, with canvas bags strapped on their chests, but it was to the man at the table that I spoke.

The talk had stopped as I rushed in. 'There's been a bomb!' I said, jerkily, short of breath. 'The houses on the north of the square have all fallen down!'

The man looked at his book. 'Thank you for reporting it, son,' he said. 'But there's been no bomb there. Off with you now, we've got work to do.'

My head spun. 'Come and look, quickly, and you'll see,' I said.

Wearily he said, 'Look, son, there's been no bomb there. Those houses were shaken to bits last month; they were barely still standing. All that's happened is that the blast's shaken a bit more of them down. Nothing to worry about. Now if you don't mind . . .'

'But . . .' I said, 'but you've got to come. Someone's got to dig her out!'

'All right, son, calm down,' he said. 'There wasn't anyone in them. They weren't safe.'

It was like the worst nightmare of my life. 'There was!' I cried. 'We were there, and I just went out

157

for some milk for Dickie, and when I got back they were under it all . . .'

'Whose sector is it?' said the man in charge. His voice had lost that weary note. He spoke sharply.

'Jack's,' someone said.

'Where is he?'

'Just coming now,' they said, pushing a newcomer to the front.

'Those houses north of the square have folded, and this kid says there were people in one of them. Were there?'

'No,' said Jack. 'Not a soul. I cleared them all out the day after the bomb made them shaky.'

'Oh, God!' I cried. 'Come and dig her out!'

'Shut up, you!' he said to me, fiercely. 'Keep a hold on yourself. Now, exactly where did you say you were living?'

'In the basement of number twenty.'

'Why didn't you report to the warden, in the proper manner?'

'I didn't know we had to,' I said, and that was true enough.

'Jack, could this kid have kipped down there, without your noticing him?'

'It's possible . . . I suppose . . .' Jack looked very uneasy. 'I *did* think I saw smoke there, one day.

Couldn't find where it was coming from. Only other thing I noticed was a funny sort of handcart that appeared at: the back of the houses the other day. I didn't think it warranted a report.'

'You'll hear from me later!' said the chief, picking up his phone.

They weren't going to believe me. I turned tail, and ran out of the hut, ran back towards the house. The black horror of it made me shake all over, but I got back to the house. I clambered up the mound of ruin to the top, and crying to myself, began to scrabble in it with my bare hands. Foul pinkish dust rose in a cloud around me, to join that already hanging in the air. My nails broke off, painfully, below the quicks. I still thrust my bleeding fingers frantically down into the mess, pulling at fragments of brick and tile, succeeding only in making a hole as big as a kitchen bucket.

'Hey, kid!' yelled someone from below me, on the street. The warden from the post had set up a red lamp on a tripod down there, and now was climbing up towards me, with a blue cover on his helmet marked *Incident Officer*.

Still on my hands and knees I scraped the ruin. He came right up, and stood over me. 'Where are your parents?' he said.

'We were on our own,' I said, sobbing a bit, in spite of myself.

'Right,' he said, calmly, as though that deserved no comment at all. 'Now listen hard. You've got to calm down, and stop going off the deep end like that, because WE NEED YOUR HELP. Got it?'

I was sober at once, as though he had doused me down with cold water. I stood up, and looked at him.

'That's better,' he said. 'Now. How many people are there in there?'

'Two,' I said. 'A girl and a very small boy.'

'Where were they?'

I looked helplessly round the featureless desert which we stood on. A lorry pulled up at the lamp below. It was full of men in navy siren-suits, and tin hats painted with R on the front, tools, timber props, and ropes. Behind it came an ambulance. The leader of the rescue squad climbed up to join us.

'There were two rooms and a passage,' I said. 'They were in the front room, and they would have been near the fire, so they would have been over to the right, somewhere there.'

'Are you sure they would have been near the fire?' asked the warden.

'Dickie was ill. He needed warmth. That's the best guess I can make.'

'Good. Well, you're quite sensible when you try. Keep it up.'

'Did you have a lighted fire?' asked the squad leader.

I nodded, and he made a gloomy grimace that stabbed me with fear.

'Go and get your hands seen to,' said the warden. 'The stretcher party will do that for you. And stick around, we may need you.' As I went I heard him say, 'Not too good?'

'Tricky,' said the rescue man. 'But I've seen worse.'

The girls driving the ambulance had a doctor with them. He cleaned up my fingers and put bandages round them.

'You're a bit shaken,' he told me. 'We'll send you off for a rest.'

'I have to stay here,' I said. 'They said they might need me.' He made me sit on a bunk in the ambulance, and put a blanket round me. As soon as he turned his back I got out of there, for I couldn't bear not to see what was going on.

They had long metal rods, and they were probing with them, driving them in every few inches over the mound. Then they stopped that, and said that a tunnel wouldn't be safe.

'We'll have to get it off the top,' the leader said. At once they brought baskets, shovels and picks. They began to shovel rubble into baskets, and making a chain across the mound, they handed the loaded baskets from one to another, down the mound, and tipped the stuff into the street.

I felt very shaky. Still wrapped in my blanket I sat on the step that led to the driver's cab of the lorry, and just watched. An icy wind was blowing under a grey sky. The whole world was grey, dirty. Dirt blowing in the wind. I felt as though my mouth was full of ashes, and a great weight was pressing on my eyes.

They worked hard. They didn't talk, they just grunted to one another. Now and then they changed places, not to take a rest, but just to do a different job. They had moved a hell of a lot of debris in an hour. The dump pile in the street was growing massive, and I thought they must be getting somewhere, when suddenly they set up cries of alarm, and began to slither and scramble down. The whole mass of the fallen house was shifting, moving, the shape changing like a sleeper moving under a blanket, and a great avalanche of rubble slid and roared down onto the place they had cleared.

They gathered in a tight little circle in the street, conferring. Just then a W.V.S. van drove up, and brisk ladies began to ply them with soup and tea and cheese sandwiches. The men stood around, eating, eyeing the job as they stood. Their chiefs still talked together. Someone offered me a bowl of soup, and I nearly screamed at her.

'I can't eat while she's under there!'

Then I heard one of the rescue squad say, 'Here, let me try.' He took my soup, and came and squatted on the ground in front of me. 'You eat up, son. It's cold, and this is going to be a long job, and we need you, still in a state to help, later on, when we get somewhere.' I took the soup. I looked at him. He had a weatherbeaten face, wrinkled at the corners, and he was very dirty. His hands, cupped round his own mug of tea, were wide, and the hairs on the backs of them were whitened with pale dust.

'Are you going to get to her?' I asked him.

He looked back at me with very blue eyes. 'Yes. We always get there, in the end.'

'Will she be all right?' I screwed up my eyes in agony, vainly trying to block out the crushed and broken images in my mind. He was answering;

'Could be. Last week we dug out an old lady, what had been under for three days; three *days*, mind you. We had a nice canvas bag, all ready for her. When we gets to her, she sits up, smartly, like a Judy in a show, up she comes, swearing the place blue, because we hadn't reached her sooner!'

Someone called to him. They were starting work again. This time they worked differently. They brought wooden props, and lengths of tarpaulin, and made supports to hold back the wall of rubble. They cleared a much wider space, and so it was much slower. It was three hours before they got back down again to the tangle of timbers where the floor, the basement ceiling had been. All that time I sat there. It went through my mind that if I had let her go back to her parents when she read about the ship going down, she would be warm and safe somewhere now. But I didn't really feel anything. I was numb to the core. Numb with cold, numb with fear.

They brought me several cups of tea during that time; I drank them, but I didn't really want to thaw out. Then they were sawing, the rasping noise zig-zagging through the square – then they were carrying away beams and rafters so tangled that they looked like crumpled straws. Then at last a voice called, 'Is that kid still there?'

164

I clambered up to them. They were standing on a web of broken timber. They had made a hole through it, and below was another layer of dust and rubble.

'Look,' they said. 'These blackened bricks are from the chimney. So if the chimney's here, how far over do we try, to get to the middle of the room?'

I closed my eyes. I tried to remember the size of the room. 'It's a big room,' I said. 'But there was a table in it, so the free space wasn't in the middle.'

'If she was in the middle of the free space when it happened, about how far over from the chimney?' he asked. I noticed vaguely that he spoke gently to me.

'About here,' I said, shuddering at the thought. 'Just where I'm standing.'

'Right. You go and stand over there, by those props. Get going, squad.'

I stood back, poised against the tarpaulin dam, and watched them. Swirls of dust raised from the rubble wound round them like fog. They brought shovels and spades, and more baskets.

Down in the street I saw the stretcher party, white-helmeted, standing ready. My heart beat so that the pressure of it hurt me. Then it took almost no time at all. They swung their heavy spades into the rubble, and stood on the flanges, leaning their weight on them, before lifting a spadeful away; and then someone cried, 'Steady on! I've found a hand here,' and they all stopped. They stood back. Three of them, on hands and knees, leant down, and scooped the dust away tenderly, with bare hands.

And slowly, handful by handful, a shape appeared. She had been buried standing up, and they were uncovering her face.

A face of stone. Plaster, crushed to powder, covered her hair and skin. Her hair was stiff, grey. A grainy texture, like weathered marble, covered her cheeks; her lashes were loaded with dust, thickened by it, as though they had been fretted from the coarse substance of stone. They uncovered her shoulders, part of her body. Her attitude was stiff; statuesque, she stood rigid, with one hand extended in front of her. She had been turned to stone. She looked like one of those angels of death which stand on tombstones, slowly crumbling with weather and time. I watched a stream of tiny particles of dust flow down her cheek from the laden strands of her hair.

It began to rain then. The rescue men were

working their way around her, trying to release her legs. The rain fell. The foul smell of wet plaster rose from the mess. The rain splashed her upturned cheeks like tears, cleaned her face, like cold tears, showing the smooth pale flesh beneath the dirt.

And suddenly there came back to me – as she had said words came back to her, much later – forgotten words, once meaningless, that went through my mind like naked flame:

Oh, western wind, when wilt thou blow,
The small rain down can rain,
Christ, that my love were in my arms,
And I in my bed again.

But she is there. That limp form, whose arm hangs down all wrong, being lifted clear now, laid down on a stretcher, covered, carried away.

I flung back my head, and howled, like a dog, at the sky.

The ambulance doctor struck me in the face, first on one cheek, then on the other, not angrily, coolly and carefully, just as he had dressed my hands. I shut up. They pushed me forwards. There was a big hole now, a hollow space under the shattered flooring, and a rescue man was crawling around down there.

'We don't know where to look for the other one,' he said. 'You got a guess?'

'She was holding him,' I said dazedly.

'Not when it happened.'

'Well, if she had put him down, it would have been in one of the chairs, very near the fire, I should think. Over that way a bit.'

He disappeared into the hole, and came back with a scrap of green fabric, held it up to me over his upturned face.

'This from the chair?' he asked. I nodded. Back he went.

On a sudden impulse I stepped forwards, and slithered down into the hole with him. It seemed a long way down. There was a gap between the sagging rafters and the floor, just enough to crawl through. 'The other chair would have been this way,' I said, crawling towards it myself.

He came with me. The chair back was propping up cracked rafters. He shone his torch at it, and we could just see a bump, covered with plaster, in the seat of the chair. Together we pulled at it, and the blanket came off in our hands, and there underneath it was Dickie, asleep, quite clean, and unharmed, Edging forwards I put my arms round him, and pulled him out, going backwards on hands and knees till we reached the hole again, and could stand up. I looked upwards through a ring of foreshortened men, standing on the rim of the hole, their tin hats circling a patch of sky through which the rain still fell. From all directions hands reached down to help us up. They rolled Dickie in a blanket, and took him off to the ambulance. They picked up their picks and shovels, and moving slowly, tiredly, they gathered round their lorry in the street and began to climb in. The ambulance moved off, the warden took down his lamp, and waved to the squad in the lorry.

I just stood there. It was getting dark, slowly, the rain blurring the margins of night and day. Suddenly one of the rescue squad, the one who had got me to drink some soup, called down to me:

'Cheer up, mate! Don't stand there like you 'adn't enough to do!'

'There's nothing for me to do,' I said, flatly.

'Well, if I was you,' he said, 'I'd get a bite to eat, and some kip, and then go and ask at the hospital about that girlfriend of yours. Or is she your sister?'

'*Hospital?*' I said. I suppose the look on my face told him what I was thinking.

'Cripes!' he said, as the lorry started up. 'We oughter 'ave told 'im.' The lorry began to move. 'She was alive, mate,' he called back to me where I stood. 'We got her out alive!'

9

I began to walk, in a daze of weariness and hope, towards the nearest hospital. I remember being so tired that there was a swimming sensation in my head, and the stars appearing in the darkening sky spun like tops in my eyes. When I reached the hospital, I found I could hardly push open the revolving doors; I had to lean my whole weight against them, instead of turning them with an extended hand. Inside, in a brown lobby, a woman sat behind glass, writing.

I went and stood there, and she looked up and said, 'Casualty entrance is at the back.' I couldn't think what she meant. She said it again. Looking vaguely around, I suddenly saw a dim reflection of myself in a glass door. I was indescribably ragged and filthy, and of course my hands were bandaged with grimy gauze.

'Can you get there on your own?' she asked. A faint expression of concern had dawned on her face.

'I'm not a casualty,' I managed to say. 'I want to see someone, someone who was brought in today.'

'Young man,' she said, dryly, 'Whether you think you are a casualty or not, you certainly look like one to me. Nurse Hobbs!' she had called a passing nurse, and then of course, I was being marched down a corridor towards Casualty.

'There's nothing wrong with me,' I told them. 'I've come to see someone.'

'Like that?' they enquired, disbelievingly. 'No nonsense now, do what you're told.' So I sat down and had my hands unwrapped. The doctor picked up my hands, looked at the broken nails, said, 'That's not much to write home about,' in the scornful voice of one used to dealing with better things, and handed me over to a nurse. She put clean dressings on me.

'You look as if you badly need some sleep,' they told me. 'We'll send you home in an ambulance.'

172

'I'm bombed out,' I said.

'To a Rest Centre, then,' they said.

'I want to see someone before I go,' I protested, but they wouldn't have it, saying I needed sleep first, and I felt too weak to argue much, so off I went.

It was a good Rest Centre, much better than the last one we had been in. They found me a tub of hot water to clean up in, and new clothes, quite good ones really, that fitted better than the Salvation Army Mission's jacket; but it cost me a pang to see that jacket drop into the waste bin just the same. There were wire bunks to sleep in, and when I had eaten a little I lay down; just for half an hour, I thought, and then I will go and find her. But when I woke it was the next day. It was light, and I was already too late for breakfast. They kept asking me questions there, about who I was, and where I would be going, and I had to tell a pack of lies before I could get away, and set off again for that hospital.

Once more a woman sat behind glass there, writing. 'I want to see someone who was brought in yesterday,' I said. She didn't look up, so I said it again.

'Very well, then, who is it you want to see?' she said.

173

'Julie. Julie something, but I don't know what.'

'*That* isn't much help then, is it?' she snapped. 'And you can't be a relative, or much of a friend if you don't even know her name.' I stood there. 'Do you know what she was in for?' she asked.

'She'd been buried,' I said, overcome by an awful cut-off feeling.

'Wait a minute, and I'll look at the list,' she said. 'No . . . sorry . . . No Julie admitted this week. She isn't here. You'd better try somewhere else. Unless . . . Julia Vernon-Greene, admitted with shock, broken collar bone and abrasions. Could that be it?'

I shook my head. That didn't sound right. I went out onto the street. I thought hard. Where was the nearest hospital, other than this? I walked. I had no money now, only a shilling they had found in my jacket pocket, before sending it off to be burned, so walking it had to be.

I walked all day. I succeeded in trying nine hospitals before dark, and I didn't find her. I spent my shilling on chips for supper, and I slept in the Underground, cold, blanketless, miserable and uncomfortable. In a strange way I didn't exactly mind that; I wanted to be cold and hungry till I found her. Not being with her, not knowing how she was: had become a pain as sharp as toothache somewhere in my chest, and getting cramp on draughty concrete platforms in some mysterious manner eased the inner pain.

I felt very light-headed the next day. I walked some more, asked at a few more hospitals, but not in the desperate haste that had driven me the day before. Sometime around midday I thought I would try St Thomas's, even if it was on the far side of the river. Perhaps that awful raid had filled up all the nearer hospitals, and they had taken here there . . . I set off towards Westminster Bridge. And on the way there, outside the gates of the Embankment Gardens, by the Temple Station, I suddenly saw Marco.

He had a little cart with him, the sort you wheel by hand, with sandwiches on it, and a vast brass samovar of tea. He was wrapped up against the cold in a shabby brown greatcoat, and he was holding out both hands, and yelling with joy at seeing me.

'Amico! Amico!' he cried. 'You no come, you no come at all. And then the place all go caput, and you not know where to come. You are hungry, no? I give you good food; look, you like cheese? You like cucumber? And where is Miss Julia? You tell Marco all about it.'

I shook my head. 'She's in hospital, and I can't find her,' I said. 'And I can't have any food, Marco, I'm afraid. I'm sorry, but I haven't any money.'

'Did Marco ask you for the money?' he said. 'You Marco's good friend. You eat some food now, drink some tea.' I hesitated. 'You a good boy,' he said. 'I know that. You never call me dirty I-tie, not like some. I can give some food for my friend, no?'

And as soon as I started to eat, I realized that the light-headed feeling was hunger; I could feel it going away with every mouthful I got into my stomach. As the hot tea got down there, I really began to feel myself again, and a thought began to form in my head. It was Marco who had reminded me – he had said, 'Miss Julia.' Hadn't she looked a little startled to be called that, once? Could she have called herself Julie to make herself sound more ordinary, just as I had told het my name was Bill? If only I had asked her her name, or read that disc of hers properly! The disc! With her number on – of course! Her number. I knew her number!

I thanked Marco, and set off with the wind in my heels for the hospital I had first tried; I burst through the revolving door at about twenty miles an hour, and rushed up to the desk.

'I want to see someone called Julie . . .' I began.

'Oh, it's you again, is it?' The receptionist was annoyed. 'I thought I looked, and she wasn't here.'

'Her number,' I said. 'I've remembered her number. Please look again.' I thought I was about to be let in, to run up those stairs, and be laughing with Julie again, and my voice bubbled with excitement.

'Julia Vernon-Greene,' she said. 'That was the only one it could have been, wasn't it?'

'Yes,' I said, 'ZKDN stroke seventy-four stroke eight.'

'That's right,' she said. 'That's her number.'

'I want to see her,' I said, joyfully.

'Sorry. No visitors.'

'What do you mean?'

'No visitors. It's against her name in the book. She's too ill to see anybody.'

'But you *must* let me see her . . .' I was bewildered. 'I'm the only person she knows, the only person she's got. You've got to let me see her!'

'Are you sure?' the woman said. 'Well, in that case, let me have your name, and then just wait here while I go and see. There's a seat there.'

I sat there. The hospital corridor was painted dark green with a brown stripe, and then cream.

The reception lobby was painted all chocolate brown. Where the two schemes met there was an extra dark green line.

Then, just down the corridor, I heard voices breaking the antiseptic hush. The reception nurse was talking to another nurse, an important-looking nurse, with a tall starched cap, and a starch-stiff face.

'He says he's the only person in London that she knows. In that case, could he see her?'

'Nonsense!' she said, sharply, loudly, making sure I could hear. 'Julia Vernon-Greene's family have been traced. Her mother is here now. She is far too ill to receive visitors other than her family, and there is no need for any outsider to be concerned.'

The receptionist was coming back. 'Sorry, son,' she said, 'but no!'

By then, so much saying she was too ill, had made a worse fear overwhelm me; perhaps she was dying . . . perhaps the falling house had done awful things to her, broken her . . .

'How ill is she, really?' I asked, in a hoarse voice. My voice was thick with tears. I couldn't help it, there I was, crying. In theory crying isn't so bad – a way of expressing deep feelings. But when one

178

is really doing it, it's all the things that go with it that make one ashamed – having a wet nose, and a shake in one's voice, and a smeary feeling on burning cheeks.

The receptionist's face swam above me. 'It's shock. She badly needs a rest, and she doesn't quite know where she is, just now, but it's nothing serious, it will wear off in a day or two,' she was saying.

I recovered my self-control. 'Look when it does wear off, she'll want to see me; I know she will.'

'Well, now,' she said, not unkindly, 'Why don't you come back at visiting time tonight? You leave your name, and as soon as she's well enough, I'll see that she's asked if she wants to see you.'

'I'll wait,' I said.

'It's a long time,' she said. 'It's only half past three. But I suppose that's all right, as long as you keep out of the way.'

So I waited. All that day. Nurses walked by me, and doctors in white coats. Once a patient was wheeled by on a trolley. Most of them glanced at me as they passed. I stared at them – a change from facing with vacant eyes the borders of the areas of paint. Sometime around five there was an air-raid warning outside. The receptionist reached up – took off her white cap, and put on a tin hat instead. 'Time crawled on. About an hour after the air-raid warning an ambulance, ringing wildly, drew into the yards outside; nurses and doctors ran; their feet clattering grotesquely loudly down quiet corridors. A trolley loaded with bottles and kidney-shaped trays was wheeled past me at a run. One of its wheels squeaked. Then more time, more looking at paint.

Visitors began to arrive. After hours of looking at white-aproned, white-coated people moving in drab-painted places, the visitors struck me as very coloured. Their clothes seemed garish, like the middle pages of a comic. And the quiet of the place had not yet reached them, so they talked to each other, quite loudly. They brought grapes in cellophane wrappings, and bunches of flowers, and books. They were let in to see their friends. It occurred to me that anyone of them might be Julie's family, being let in to see *her*. Hating them, I lowered my eyes and glowered at my boots as they passed me.

Considering what they had been through, my boots were in quite good shape. They hadn't let in water yet; the Dubbin had been worth it. Dimly it occurred to me to wonder if Mrs Williams had been worried about me; not that she could have cared much. It couldn't be anything like worrying about Julie was for me. Even so I felt a tenderness for any feeling like that, however pale a shadow of my own. When I had seen Julie, I would send Mrs Williams a postcard.

A bell rang; visiting time was over. People trooped out. The nurse said to me, 'Go home now. You'll have to go now. Try again tomorrow.' I got up, stiff with sitting so long, and went out. It was dark outside, and cold. I went to find a shelter to sleep in.

I slept so little that night, was so cold and so lonely, that I came up again into the streets, very early, and walked about in the grey light, hoping that walking would thaw my cramped limbs. There had been more bombing in the night. I remember seeing the usual mess and chaos, but though I saw I hardly noticed. I climbed up Hungerford Bridge, and stood on the footbridge, looking down over the Embankment, seeing the grey road under a grey sky, seeing grey water through the branches of bare black trees. The cold dawn in the east was casting a cold light, and the tram-lines below me shone sleekly in the tarmac. I wondered what I would do. I wondered where she would be; where they would take her. I thought the paper said there would be no more boats to Canada, but unless she was going to stay in London, things could well be nearly as bad. I would have to go and get my cart, and do some work again, sometime . . . no, I hadn't the heart for that; as soon as I thought about it, I knew I couldn't do it without her to do it for. I'd have to find my aunt. Or perhaps Julie would think of something. Perhaps she'd run away again, and come and join me.

At nine I went back to my seat in the hospital corridor. Time crawled. A uniformed delivery boy came in with a huge bunch of flowers, and said, 'Miss Vernon-Greene'. I watched them intently, out of the corner of my eye, pretending not to notice. After a while a porter came by, and the receptionist pointed to them, and said, 'Room Nine'. He picked up the flowers and went off. She wasn't looking at me. I got up, and slipped along the passage. I looked at the notices at the foot of the flights of stairs. 'Wards one to five' 'Wards five to nine'. Up I went. Up three flights. Turn right, my heart in my mouth, in case someone stopped me . . . I opened the door. The ward was wrecked. The roof had been blown off, the beds were broken and twisted, debris was spread across the floor, and broken glass and furniture. A piece of roof tarpaulin over the hole in the ceiling flapped in the wind. There was no nobody there. I climbed slowly down the stairs. Hadn't she said Ward Nine?

At about twelve o'clock I was feeling light in the head again, and so I went and found Marco, and shamefacedly let him feed me. I told him what had happened this time, and he flooded me with sympathy. He said I could help him with the sandwiches, and he would give me a little money when he could manage it. Then one day, when the war was over, we would have a little restaurant, and call it 'Marco and Bill's Cosmopolitan Snack Bar'. He raised a faint smile on my stiff face, but I shook my head. 'I can't even fry an egg, Marco. I'd be no use to you.'

Then back again to wait. This time I plucked up courage to ask at the desk how she was getting on, and if they had asked her about me yet. They said she was getting on nicely. That's all they would say.

Then, at long last, that evening, when the visitors had all been let in, a nurse came down, and said to the receptionist, 'Miss Vernon-Greene is asking if someone called Bill has been asking for her.' My heart leapt. I stood up, and she was pointing to me. 'You may come up,' the nurse said, and I followed her, barely able to keep myself from running ahead, and up we went, and I thought, I will be with her, any moment, any moment now . . .

It was Room Nine, not Ward Nine. The nurse opened the door, and I rushed in, so hastily that I bumped into the bottom of the bed, and stood there . . . She was sitting up in bed, smiling at me. They had cut off her hair, and bandaged her head. A few fronds of dark hair, roughly hacked off, showed under the bandage, round her face. She looked pale, and I could see, still visible, the faint mark of the bruise I had made on her lip when the blast wave caught us. But in the same moment I saw that we were not alone. There was a strange woman sitting beside her, wearing a brown hat, holding her hand. And behind me, as I looked round, a tall young man, so like her that I knew at once she had a brother, rose to his feet. He seemed to be wearing some sort of uniform, a blazer with a crest, and a striped tie. She hadn't said she had a brother . . .

'Hullo, Bill,' she said. 'Mother, this is Bill. Bill, this is my brother, Robin.'

'Oh,' I said. Then, after too long a pause,

'Hullo.' I looked at her. She looked at me, but then looked away. Her mother looked out of the window.

'Did they tell you about Dickie?' she asked, suddenly. I hadn't given Dickie a thought from the moment they dug him out, 'They've got him here, and he isn't hurt, but they can't find his mother, and . . .' Her voice started to shake.

'Come now, Julia, don't upset yourself,' said her mother. 'What can't be helped has to be put up with, dear.'

'I'm glad he wasn't hurt,' I said.

'They let him see me,' she said.

'Oh,' I said, stabbed with jealousy,

'Are you all right?' she said.

'Yes, thank you.' I couldn't think of anything to say to her. There was nothing to say that I wanted a woman in a brown hat, and a sleek young man to hear.

'Is the cart doing well?' she asked, in the thickening silence.

'Don't know. Haven't tried.' I was almost mumbling. My eye was caught by a glint of silver on her bedside table – my little Spitfire lay there, half concealed under a bunch of grapes in cellophane, and towered over by a vase of flowers.

Suddenly Robin spoke. 'Oh, er, look here, er, Bill . . .' he was saying. 'Since my father isn't here, you know, I think I ought to say . . . Well, look, my sister's far too young to have well, friends outside the family, you know, but since in the circumstances . . . well, since you looked after her we can't very well forbid you . . . we could make an exception, if . . . well, if you can give me your word that there isn't anything in it.'

I knew what he was getting at. Anger flashed through me. I opened my mouth to say, '*Go to hell!*' and '*I'll see her if I want to see her, without asking you!*' when Julie spoke, first.

'Oh, Robin, don't be *silly!*' she said. '*Of course* there's nothing in it, nothing at all.'

'Oh, well, good. All right, then,' he said.

Julie's mother, looking at me with an odd sort of expression, said, 'I think Robin only wants to thank you, Bill . . .'

But I was looking at Julie.

Then I turned abruptly, and went. I ran down the corridor, and ran, scrambling down the flights of stairs, and I felt as if I were falling, falling, down them. At the bottom a trolley was being wheeled along the corridor, and I couldn't push past it, to get out of there. I rushed past the receptionist, as soon as the trolley let me by, and put out my hands for the turning door, when there was Julie's mother, who had followed and overtaken me.

'Bill,' she said. 'Don't take any notice of Robin. He meant to thank you for looking after Julia so bravely. If you would like to come and see us at our house at Richmond, we should be delighted to receive you there.' She had a lovely smooth even voice. She held out a small white card with an address printed on it. 'Will you come?'

Dumbly I shook my head.

She looked at me again with that oddly sympathetic expression, and said, 'You know, Bill, she's only a child.'

I closed my eyes and leaned back against the door, and it turned, like a roundabout, and threw me out into the night.

I could not walk, I could only run, driven by the angry grief within me as leaves are driven by the wind; poor draggled leaves, lashed by the driving wind. They wrapped round my ankles as I ran, overtook me, and dropped down in front of me. Through and through my head went her voice, saying *of course there's nothing in it, nothing at all.* Soon I ran out of breath, and stood, gasping the raw cold air, watching the leaves go on without me on the wind. O western wind, when wilt thou blow. O western wind . . .

10

I thought being dead would be a good way out. I remembered the fire-watcher on Hungerford Bridge, dead, with reflected fire in his eyes. So I went to a fire station, and volunteered. They did ask me how old I was, but when I lied they seemed to believe me. They gave me a tin hat, and a lot of instructions, and sent me up on to the roof of a big office block in the Strand, to sit beside a field telephone and watch.

I discarded the tin hat at once, and I waited for death to rain down on me, eagerly, with longing. That was the night of November the twenty-third; the first night for fifty-seven nights that there were no raids on London at all. So there I was, all night long, quite safe, under the shining stars.

In the morning I tried another way; I went off to volunteer for the army. I only had to give myself a year or two extra to be taken on as a trainee cadet in the Engineers. Perhaps I would learn enough to be an engineer after all. There were a lot of other fellows there, smiling, and exchanging names, and one in particular I liked the look of, called Ronnie. He was standing next to me when we stripped down for the medical, and all across his back was a livid purple scar nearly an inch wide.

'Whatever happened to your back, Ronnie?' I asked him.

''That?' he said, grinning. 'That was a bit of me Dad's greenhouse, with a bomb behind it. It's my war-wound that is. How about you; you got a war-wound?'

'Me?' I said. 'Nothing. Not a scratch.'

Years later, when the war was over and done with, it occurred to me that she might not have meant what she said. Perhaps she only said it as a sort of cover, to shut him up, and make sure we *could* go on seeing each other. I hope that's what she meant, because I hate to think she was the sort who might just make use of someone, and then chuck them; I hope that's what she meant for her sake, though it's too late now to make any difference to me, either way. I wonder why I didn't think of it at the time.

I think of it now, leaning on a broken wall, looking at St Paul's. You can see it much better now that everything round it has been knocked down. All around me there are open acres, acres of ruined and desolate land, where the bombs fell. Over there the square tower of a gutted church survives as the only landmark, till the harmonious walls of the cathedral rise exposed in the background. It's quiet here, and beautiful, for into this wilderness the wild things have returned. Grass grows here, covering, healing, and russet sorrel in tall spikes, and goldenrod, swaying beside broken walls, full of butterflies, and purple loosestrife, and one plant, willow herb, that some people call fireweed, grows wild in this stony place as plentifully as grass, though it used to be rare enough to be searched out, and collected. It is a strange plant; it has its own rugged sort of loveliness, and it grows only on the scars of ruin and flame.

I suppose they will build on this again, some day: but I like it best like this; grown over; healed.

Jill Paton Walsh

Jill Paton Walsh was born Gillian Bliss in London in 1937. Jill has won several awards, including the Whitbread Prize, the Boston Globe-Horn Book Award, the Universe Prize, and the Smarties Grand Prix. In 1970 FIREWEED won the Book World Festival Award, and her adult novel KNOWLEDGE OF ANGELS was nominated for the 1994 Booker Prize. After living for many years in Surrey, she is now settled in Cambridge. In 1996 she received the CBE for services to literature, and was elected a fellow of the Royal Society of Literature. Visit Jill at her website: www.greenbay.co.uk/jpw.html